GRETA ZARGO

AND THE AMOEBA MONSTERS FROM THE MIDDLE OF THE EARTH

A.F. HARROLD

ILLUSTRATED BY
JOE TODD-STANTON

BLOOMSBURY
CHILDREN'S BOOKS

LONDON OXFORD NEW YORK NEW DELHI SYDNEY

BLOOMSBURY CHILDREN'S BOOKS
Bloomsbury Publishing Plc
50 Bedford Square, London, WC1B 3DP, UK

BLOOMSBURY, BLOOMSBURY CHILDREN'S BOOKS and the Diana logo
are trademarks of Bloomsbury Publishing Plc

First published in Great Britain in 2018 by Bloomsbury Publishing Plc

A catalogue record for this book is available from the British Library

ISBN: PB: 978-1-4088-8177-4; eBook: 978-1-4088-8178-1

2 4 6 8 10 9 7 5 3 1

Typeset by RefineCatch Limited, Bungay, Suffolk

Printed and bound in Great Britain by CPI Group (UK) Ltd, Croydon CR0 4YY

To find out more about our authors and books visit www.bloomsbury.com
and sign up for our newsletters

For Mabel Yates

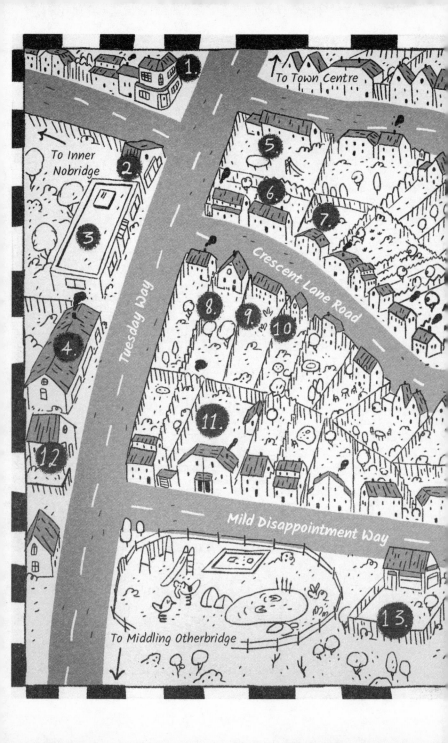

Outer Eastbridge

Lower Upperbridge

Inner Nobridge

Middling Otherbridge

Upper Lowerbridge

N W E S

1. Doodad's Shop
2. Dry Cleaner
3. Snorkel Supply Shop
4. Harp Shop
5. The Appledumps
6. Aunt Tabitha
7. Mr. Borris
8. Greta Zargo
9. Brigadier Ryefoot-fforwerd
10. Jessica Plumb
11. Mr and Mrs Jamali
12. Mr Teachbaddly
13. Wet Cleaner
14. The Cohens
15. The Merridews
16. Mrs Hummock

To the Toothpaste Mines →

Upper Lowerbridge & Environs

PROLOGUE

Untold Miles Beneath the Earth's Crust

WEDNESDAY, FIVE MONTHS AGO

SOMETHING HAD BEEN woken. Something ancient. Something unnamed. Something that should not have been woken.

Deep in the Earth. Beneath the deepest well, below the deepest mine, further down than the deepest potholer's pothole. It was deep down there, down where the sleepers had slept for untold ages.

1

Deep. Dark. Hot. Silent.

And then ...

scrunch,   scrunch, scrunch

... the spade came digging.

A simple electric spade that had been invented by a kindly aunt to help one little girl with her garden-ing, and now ... it had dug *too deep.**

Things that had dwelt in dark-ness, chewing rocks slowly, had their world cracked open.

* It had dug too deep because no one could find the remote control with the 'off' button on it.

And they began to climb, inching slowly up the shaft, squeezing stickily between sheer, muddy rock walls.

Above them a new world waited.

They knew nothing of sunlight, but soon they would feel it.

They knew nothing of fresh air, but soon they would taste it.

They knew nothing of people, but soon they would eat them.

And so they climbed, and above them the world slept, unaware of the horror that approached, unaware of the threat rising from the depths, unaware that the final end had begun.

Now read on …

CHAPTER ONE

Greta Zargo's House, Upper Lowerbridge, England, Earth

LAST SATURDAY (BREAKFAST TIME)

WHEN GRETA ZARGO'S parents accidentally died, she was left the family home, everything in it, a large bank account, two black-and-white posters of kittens falling over, a lifetime subscription to *Paperclip World* (*the* magazine for all paperclip enthusiasts) and a pair of trousers she'd one day grow into. Since she had only been a baby at the time of the accident, all this was held in trust by her Aunt Tabitha until Greta's eighth birthday.*

As soon as she turned eight, Greta moved out of her aunt's house and into her own one, just over the road. Naturally her aunt kept an eye on Greta, as often as she could, and in the three years that followed, absolutely no disasters had occurred. Other than perhaps that one time when the seagulls stole Mr Borris's wig and he wrote an outraged letter to the President about it. But even then, as Greta pointed out in a stiffly worded article in the school newspaper, it *was* a very funny-looking wig, and the President had never actually replied to Mr Borris anyway.* So no disasters at all. None.

* This rather early age for independence was due to a legally binding spelling mistake ('eighth' where it should have said 'eighteenth') in her parents' Last Will and Testament.

* Although the President of Britain, Aethelred Slightly, had been at school with Mr Borris many years before, Mr Borris tended to overestimate how memorable and, indeed, how likeable he'd been as a child.

This morning Greta was up early. It was the first day of the autumn half-term holiday and she was grumpy. Grumpy because the sun had barely made an effort outside the window to warm the world. Grumpy because the only clean socks she had were yesterday's dirty ones. And grumpy because of the general awful earliness of the getting up.

Greta believed that the holidays were not the time for early rising. To be fair, she didn't think school days were for early rising either, but the Head had sent her home with so many letters to give to herself, asking her to make sure she was at school on time, that most days she arrived at school *almost* in time to not quite be told off. (Other children would have been given letters addressed to their parents, but, for obvious reasons, that

7

didn't work for Greta. She was, legally, acting *in loco parentis* for herself, which just means she was her own mother and father, so far as letters home went.)

Grumpily Greta made herself breakfast and grumpily she got dressed and grumpily she went out the back door, scowling at the grey day and pulling her coat around her as the fog swam its damp tendrils across the garden.

Grumpily she lifted her bike up from the lawn and stared at the cat that sat on the bird table.

It was a right proper nuisance that cat. It sang. At night.

In fact, to call it singing was to be overly kind to the cat. It was more of a strangled yodel that sounded like someone was passing an electric current through a group of

Norwegian goatherds who'd just been passing round a helium balloon.

And the singing wasn't even the worst thing about the cat. At least you *knew* that once the sun had gone down, the yodel would soon be coming: it wasn't exactly a surprise, and it was the cat's surprises that Greta hated most.

It had a habit of sneaking into her house and hiding dead mice in her knicker drawer.

When she wasn't expecting it.

That was the thing she hated most.

But, as a proverb her aunt had invented went: *Cats do as cats do and there's nothing to do about cats doing what they do, so you'd best accept it and move on and try not to make eye contact and, to be honest, I prefer squirrels, Greta, much friendlier on the whole and ... oh ... Are these salt and vinegar crisps?* It wasn't a great proverb – her aunt had got distracted halfway through making it – but, luckily, inventing proverbs was only a very small part of what Aunt Tabitha did.

Greta gave the cat a grumpy glower, opened the gate and pedalled off in the direction of elsewhere, without once looking back.

(Had she looked back she might've seen, through the fog and beyond the cat, the shape of something large and wobbly and jellyish, pulsating on the grass beside the deep hole at the far end of the garden. But since she didn't look back, and since the fog was swirling, she didn't see it, and since the large, wobbly, jellyish thing didn't have any eyes, it didn't see her either, and so nobody saw nothing and the memory of the thing they didn't see didn't lurk at the back of their minds all morning, niggling and troubling and wobbling.)

As Greta cycled, her grumpiness began to clear away.

Greta worked, in her spare time, as an unpaid volunteer junior reporter for *The Local Newspaper*, reporting personally to Wilfred Inglebath, the editor.* She was always looking for a Big Story that would make the front page, her name, and people gasp. And today she thought she might have one.

She pedalled through the quiet streets of Upper Lowerbridge and out of town, towards the Hester Sometimes Conference Centre and Immobile Library. It was in the conference centre Greta was due to meet her aunt, who was hosting and organising

* The Local Newspaper was an award-winning newspaper, as it boasted on the front cover. It had won the Most Expensive Free Newspaper Prize three years running, until one of the judges realised there was something wrong with the award, and it was scrapped.

the Twelfth Annual Festival of New Stuff (TAFoNS, for short).

If a whole bunch of scientists presenting the New Stuff they had made and discovered, in a converted stately home just outside Upper Lowerbridge, wasn't the sort of thing to make a great story for *The Local Newspaper*, then Greta was a haddock. Which she wasn't.*

As she turned the last corner and free-wheeled down the long, straight drive towards the Hester Sometimes Conference Centre and Immobile Library, the sun came out and the last tendrils of fog disappeared into wherever it was that fog went.*

Wheeeee, thought Greta as the wind whippled her hair.

She skidded to a halt in front of the entrance, and read half of the sign that

* She even had the paperwork to prove it if needed.

*No one knew for sure where this was. The only expedition, led in 1972 by the great poet Albert Rhymeswell, never returned from wherever it was they went.

was stuck to the automatic sliding glass doors.

She stood very still and waited for the doors to forget she was there and close themselves again, and then she read the other half of the sign.

It said: *Twelfth Annual Festival of New Stuff (TAFoNS, for short).*

Someone had added the word 'Cancelled' underneath, using a scruffy black pen

(it wasn't written in Aunt Tabitha's handwriting).

Oh, Greta thought.

Three further thoughts followed close on the heels of the *Oh*.

Firstly: *I didn't need to get up so early, after all.*

Secondly: *Well, that's my Big Story up the spout.*

And thirdly: *I'd best go find Aunt Tabitha and see what's what's what.*

CHAPTER TWO

Greta Zargo's Back Garden, Upper Lowerbridge, England, Earth

LAST SATURDAY (JUST AFTER BREAKFAST)

SLOWLY THE GELATINOUS blob slumphed its way over the edge of the hole. Bits of mud and flecks of grit writhed on its surface, like currants swirling on top of a giant transparent jellyish cake.

Not having eyes, it didn't watch as

17

Greta cycled away, but it did sense the moist mist and the whispering movement of fresh air on its outer membrane. It wobbled with mindless surprise at these new sensations*and that wobbling attracted the attentions of the cat Greta had just glowered at.

The cat was called Major Influence and he ate one in every four birds that landed in Greta's garden, even though it wasn't his garden. He wandered over to the wriggling, squirming shape that had emerged from the great hole and wondered whether it was something he could eat.

He sniffed it.

As he sniffed, the gooey blob tapped him on the nose with a small, gooey, blobby protrusion.

It was how a gelatinous thing sniffed back.

* There is very little fog or wind underground.

Major Influence jumped at the cold, oozy, strange touch, but found that his jump didn't take him nearly as far as his jump normally took him.

In fact, it didn't take him anywhere.

The thing was still touching his nose. It was stuck there.

He flipped over and began kicking at the jelly-like blob with his back legs, hissing and clawing like a furious, furry, miniature upside-down lawnmower. But ... it was no good.

Slowly, hair by hair, whisker by whisker, ear by ear, the oozing jelly blob surrounded the struggling cat until the poor thing was entirely inside it, floating helplessly in the middle of the pulsating jelly.

And then the wobbling monster paused. It sat there, pulsating and throbbing and writhing, and it began to digest its first-ever above-ground meal.

On the fence, three sparrows and an asthmatic blackbird watched with interest. They approved of the removal of Major Influence and they would have applauded, if they had hands. But they didn't. So they didn't.

From out of the great dark hole at the bottom of Greta's garden a second,

slightly larger, slightly blobbier, wobbling form began to emerge. It slowly hauled itself over the muddy lip on to the dewy lawn, and with a deep, low slurphing-slumping sound did *absolutely nothing* for a bit.

CHAPTER THREE

Hester Sometimes Conference Centre and Immobile Library, Near Upper Lowerbridge, England, Earth

LAST SATURDAY (NOT LONG AFTER BREAKFAST)

'HAVE YOU SEEN my aunt anywhere?' asked Greta, tapping her pencil on her notepad and staring up at the big, sad eyes of a white-coloured, brown-coloured cow.

She'd walked into the entrance hall of the Hester Sometimes Conference Centre and Immobile Library and gone over to the first, and only, person she'd seen, who happened to be stood next to the cow.

'I don't know,' said the man. He spoke in an accent Greta had only ever heard people speak in in films.* 'It depends, I guess, on who you think your aunt is.'

It was a fair answer, she had to admit.

Part of the point of the Twelfth Annual Festival of New Stuff (TAFoNS, for short) was that inventors and scientists from beyond the local area came to visit. This chap might never have read *The Local Newspaper* and seen her photograph beside one of her brilliant stories. To him, she might just be a little girl asking questions.

* For instance, the police officer in Hey! That Dinosaur Bit My Skateboard (2023) or the greengrocer from There Ain't No Oranges in Space (2009).

'The name's Zargo,' she said, looking him deep in the eye.* 'Greta Zargo.'

'Excuse me,' the man said as the cow, whose halter he was holding, noisily dropped a surprisingly firm looking cowpat on the chequerboard-tiled floor of the grand entrance hall.

'My aunt ...' said Greta, following him round the back end of the cow and trying to maintain eye contact, which was difficult as he turned his back on her and crouched down to look at the cow's deposit. 'My aunt is –'

'Hold this, would ya?' the man said, handing her a paper bag that he'd pulled from an inside pocket.

'Er, yes,' said Greta, tucking her notepad under her arm and her pencil behind her ear.

* The left one, which was slightly closer to her, partly because of the way his head was tilted, but mostly because his right eye was floating in a jar back home in Wyoming.

25

This interview wasn't going as well as she'd hoped.* When she'd started it, she'd expected, twenty seconds later, to be given some directions that would lead her to her aunt, not be asked to hold a paper bag while a man picked a cowpat up with a pair of metal tongs …

Which was what the man was doing.

'My aunt,' Greta began again, 'is Aunt –'

She stopped mid-sentence when the man dropped the thing he had lifted up with the tongs into the bag she was holding.

'Um …' she said.

Then she tried, 'Er …'

This was a new experience for Greta, being dumbfounded, and she didn't much like it.

Of course she had often seen Mrs Stoop-Lowly in the park picking up Samantha's poo

* Since Greta was a professional amateur volunteer journalist, she called every conversation she had an 'interview', because, as Clause Six of her parents' Last Will and Testament said: Greta, darling, do remember to listen to people every now and then. You never know when one of them might say something useful, interesting or amusing. Try to spot the difference.

26

with a little plastic bag, which was a normal thing for a person to do when a dog had done its business on the rounders pitch, but she'd never seen anyone scoop the poop of a cow before. And there had been something odd about the poop the man had picked up: it hadn't looked much like a normal cowpat. A normal pat isn't something you can pick up with tongs: it's too slick and slithery. This thing had been brown and, there were no two ways about it, burger-shaped: *More patty than pat*, she thought.*

'Thank you,' he said, taking the bag from Greta's hands.

'Hey, mister,' she said, remembering that she was an investigative reporter and not some schoolgirl standing around with her mouth open because she didn't understand

* If she hadn't been holding the paper poo bag, she'd've made a note of this thought. A good turn of phrase like that could transform an ordinary newspaper article into newspaper art.

28

everything that had just happened. 'You'd best explain what just happened.'

She tapped her notepad with her pencil in a way that said to the outside world, 'Come on, I'm waiting and I don't have all day and, by the way, what you're going to say probably isn't as interesting as all that, and I might just wander off right now and find someone more interesting to talk to if you don't start spilling the beans pretty pronto, pal.'

'Well,' the chap said, standing up straight and smiling broadly. 'What you have been privileged to witness is the solution to one of the world's great problems, little girl.'

Greta didn't like being called 'little girl' and didn't like people who called her that, but she kept her cool and said nothing. She just let the man talk about himself. He clearly enjoyed doing it. Most of the people she spoke to did.

'The name is Walbur P. Buffalo, and Simon here' – he patted the cow's flank – 'she's my proudest and finest invention. I *was* going to reveal her to the assembled ranks of scientists and inventors and they *were* going to marvel, but it seems it's time for me and Simon to just book a rocket ticket back home to the fine town of Barbecue Green, Wyoming. This here Twelfth Annual Festival of New Stuff (TAFoNS, for short)'s cancelled. The organiser's done a runner, and she's taken the keys to the main hall, so it's a no-go on the show now. Didn't you read the sign?' He patted a pocket that contained a scruffy black pen.

'Is Simon a lady cow, Mr Buffalo?' asked Greta.

'For sure she is. Finest lady cow I've ever had the honest honour to work beside.'

'Isn't Simon normally a man's name?'

'Not in Barbecue Green, Wyoming. I named Simon here after my mother, and she was named after her mother, and she was named after her mother, and she was named after her mother, and she was named after a spelling mistake.'

'Mr Buffalo, how is a cow a – and I quote – "solution to one of the world's great problems"?'

'Hamburgers,'* said Walbur P. Buffalo. 'Cruelty-free hamburgers. Simon here eats the grass, just like a normal cow, and then inside her special fifth stomach she makes burgers. Feed her more grass and she'll make more burgers, while at the same time keeping herself fit and healthy and making milkshakes if you squeeze the udders.

* Hamburgers are not made of 'ham'; they're made of beef, except for turkey burgers, which are usually made of something else.

No need to send her to the place where cows normally go to be made into hamburgers. It's so beautiful it's genius. Well, to be precise: *she's* so beautiful, and *I'm* the genius.'

Greta thought for a moment about how she could write this up for the newspaper without using any crude words.*

'You've invented a cow that poos beef burgers?' she said.

He shook the paper bag.

'You find me the kitchens, little girl, and I'll make you the best humdinging hamburger you've ever tasted.'

Greta thought about it.

She looked at her watch.

'It's a bit early for lunch,' she said, 'and I've got to find my aunt.'

Aunt Tabitha!

'Mr Buffalo,' she said, a new urgency

* This was the sort of thing journalists like Greta had to be wary of when writing their hard-hitting stories. Some readers might be easily shocked, and you don't want them to have to put the newspaper down because they're upset by the words ***** or ****** or ********** or bum.

in her voice, 'you said something about the organiser going missing … ?'

'Too right,' he said. 'Done a bunk with the keys, and probably the dinner money too. Luckily I only paid for a self-catering room, since I can get burgers and milk out of Simon.'

'My aunt, Aunt Tabitha,' Greta said, '*she's* the organiser.'

Walbur P. Buffalo looked Greta up and down and finally said, 'Well, well, well. If you ever see her again, you tell her she won't be welcome at the Thirteenth Annual Festival of New Stuff (TAFoNS, for short), which I'm sure as heck gonna be hosting in Barbecue Green, Wyoming. She's wasted my time bringing me all the way out here, and we've already missed two episodes of *Celebrity Lumberjack Dance*

Camp, which just ain't fair on gorgeous Simon here.'

Then he turned on his heel and, leading the cow by the halter, walked away, out through the automatic sliding doors and off down the drive.

So, Aunt Tabitha had gone missing.

Greta was sure she wouldn't have run off with the keys to the main hall and the dinner money; that was a crazy idea. Which meant that *something else* must have happened to Aunt Tabitha, and the only person who could find out what, was her, Greta Zargo.

This was no longer just a search for the Big Story, but a search for Aunt Tabitha. And, with any luck, the journalistic part of Greta whispered, the two would turn out to be the same thing.

CHAPTER FOUR

The Back Garden Next Door to Greta Zargo's Back Garden, Upper Lowerbridge, England, Earth

LAST SATURDAY (SOMETIME BEFORE ELEVENSES)

BRIGADIER RYEFOOT-FFORWERD (RTD) stood in the middle of his patio, stretching, hmpffing, staring and preparing himself for his usual mid-morning yawn. It was nearly ten thirty and the birds in the trees had hushed themselves in expectation, a hedgehog had woken up specially and poked her nose out from under the brambles, and Mr Jamali, whose garden backed on to the Brigadier's, was leaning out of the upstairs window with his binoculars.*

The Brigadier opened his mouth and closed his eyes and lent his head back and stuck out his tongue, and began to yawn.

It was an amazing sight.

Butterflies in the next county were caught in the long, deep, astonishing initial intake of breath.

His arms higgled above his head and vibrated in a stretch of such coiled and constrained energy that tiny crackles of lightning played across the dark serge of his uniform.

* Mrs Jamali had often told him about the Brigadier's yawn, but this was the first day Mr Jamali was home at the right time to see one for himself.

On his chest, medals rattled like a washing machine in the noisy and worrying part of its cycle.

And then …

… something transparent, huge and blobby and transparent, like an unflavoured jelly the size of a large pony,* crashed through the Brigadier's garden fence. It flumped across the wreckage and pulsated.

The birds flew away.

The hedgehog hid.

The Brigadier switched, stretched and popped into the 'noisy breathing out' stage of his great yawn, utterly oblivious.

Mr Jamali watched with a befuddled feeling. The thing looked like a large, wobbling amoeba. He'd never seen one of those before, not in Upper Lowerbridge.

And behind it, sitting on the lawn of the

* Or a small horse.

garden next door, he could see another one, slightly smaller, and that one had the skeleton of a cat floating in the middle of it. He'd never seen one of those in Upper Lowerbridge before either.

And then …

… before the Brigadier could finish his yawn (he had just reached the 'making high-pitched squeaks and pops' part, which came before the final, great 'harrumph, shake and salute'), the giant jelly-thing engulfed his right foot with a fat tentacle. A second extrusion of transparent goo lurched out from the main body of the thing and wrapped itself round the retired military man's elbow.

And quickly, over the course of not more than two or three minutes, the whole of the Brigadier was swallowed up.

Mr Jamali thought, *Oh*.

He got his mobile phone out* and rang for the police.

'The Brigadier's been engulfed by a giant amoeba monster,' he said.

'Oh dear,' said PC Delinquent, Upper Lowerbridge's resident police officer. 'I'd best come investigate.'

'You'd better hurry,' said Mr Jamali,

looking out the window and seeing the Brigadier slowly being dissolved and digested inside the wobbling blob of jelly.

CHAPTER FIVE

Hester Sometimes Conference Centre and Immobile Library, Near Upper Lowerbridge, England, Earth

LAST SATURDAY (AROUND ABOUT ELEVENSES)

OF COURSE, AUNT TABITHA *had* gone missing before. Sometimes it happened that she would get the idea for some fancy new invention and become so swept up in the excitement that she'd pop off to the shops, or to some remote island, or into the cellar without telling anyone, and she wouldn't be seen for days.

A little later, of course, Greta would get an invitation to come and see, for example, her aunt's new Sonnet Bonnet (a hat that recited Shakespeare) or the Hertichoke (an artichoke with a map of Hertfordshire on its outer skin), or to meet Mr Smith (a crab who could walk forwards and backwards), and the mystery of Aunt Tabitha's unexplained absence would be explained.

But today was different, and this was what made Greta not *worried* exactly, but a little *uncomfortable*.

While it was perfectly normal for an aunt to get caught up when inspiration arrived, it wasn't normal when she was organising and hosting a big conference for all the other inventors and scientists. That was the sort of responsibility an aunt took seriously.

Scientists and inventors love showing off their New Stuff, especially to one another.*

So where was Aunt Tabitha?

Greta had left the entrance hall and had walked down a short corridor, trying doors until she opened one that opened on to a room with someone in.

'Excuse me,' she said to the person in the room with the person in.

They were looking at a metal cabinet that was stood against one wall. It was the size of a shower cubicle, but with more knobs, buttons and lights. It seemed to be switched off, since the lights weren't lit.

'Have you seen my aunt?' Greta asked.

The figure turned to face her and she immediately recognised Yevgeny

* The public aren't always as impressed by a new invention as the inventor might like. For example, when Sophie Doodad, who ran the corner shop in Upper Lowerbridge, heard about Mr Smith, the crab that was no longer limited to walking sideways, she said, 'So?', which is just the sort of wet blanket reaction inventors dread.

47

Ticklenesser, an inventor her aunt had mentioned. He had come up with a new way of counting to eight and a deceptively simple way of detecting the colour orange. She'd been looking forward to getting an interview with him, back before the story had changed from being one of reporting on the conference to one of finding her missing aunt.

Even though she'd never met Ticklenesser before, Greta could tell it was him because of (a) the name badge he was wearing with his name on and (b) the fact that he was an octopus in a reverse diving suit.* (Her aunt had only ever mentioned one octopus who was an inventor, so Greta was sure she wasn't mistaken.)

'Your aunt?' said Ticklenesser in a quavering robotic voice that was projected

* A clockwork-robotic suit filled with seawater, to allow folk from the underwater kingdoms to explore on land.

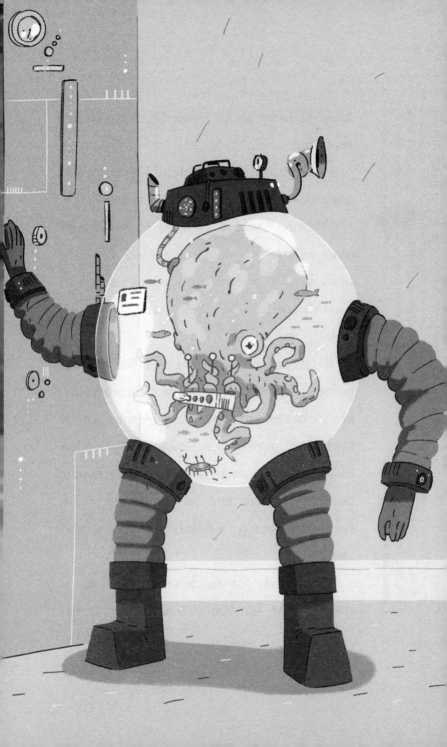

from little speakers hovering above either shoulder.

'Yes, Aunt Tabitha,' said Greta. 'She's gone missing and I'm looking for her.'

'Missing? Yes. I hear same,' said the octopus. 'She has keys to main hall. No hall, no talks. No presentations, no conference. Knowledge is lost. Aunt Tabitha is lost. Sadness swims. All is dark.'

If Greta found it strange talking to an octopus, she didn't let it show.* She watched, as Ticklenesser typed his replies on a keyboard, with two tentacle tips. One of his huge eyes, with its strange rectangular pupil, watched her as he typed. Tiny fish swam between them every now and then.

Greta said, 'Mr Ticklenesser, not only is she my aunt, but I'm also here as a repres-

* Clause Twenty-Two of her parents' Last Will and Testament said: Greta, darling, don't judge people by the colour of their hair or the shape of their feet or the number of crisps they can eat in a minute, or anything silly like that. Judge them by how they pronounce the word 'hinchworth'. This clause had puzzled Greta, especially since it gave no indication of how 'hinchworth' should be pronounced, but she tried to follow its general gist anyway.

entative of *The Local Newspaper*. If you help me, I'll mention you in my article … in fact, I'll make you a star.'

She knew she wasn't supposed to trade promises of fame for people's cooperation – that was technically called 'bribery-by-flattery' – but, well … she'd said it now.

'My name in newspaper?' said Ticklenesser. 'Octopulons* have no newspapers. Never has my name featured. Please enquire me anything, Aunt Tabitha niece.'

'When did you last see my aunt?' Greta asked, cutting to the chase.★

'I first saw Aunt Tabitha one year ago. Eleventh Annual Festival of New Stuff (EAFoNS, for short), held in my city. Great success. Many people came, displayed inventions. All declared it good. But no

* For centuries the debate about whether it should be 'octopuses' or 'octopi' had raged, but it was only when Frederika Crumble made contact with the Undersea Empire by accidentally crashing her submarine into their Museum of Kelp that the truth ('octopulons') was finally discovered.

★ Greta was an expert at cutting to the chase – everyone said so, if you gave them enough time and didn't cut to the chase before they said it.

newspapers. Too wet for newspapers, my city. Underwater, you see?'

'No,' said Greta, shaking her head, 'not when did you *first* see her. When did you *last* see her?'

'Second time I saw Aunt Tabitha,' Ticklenesser went on, 'yesterday evening. Welcomed me in this place. Curious and friendly. Talking to many inventors, giving name badges.'

He tapped a clockwork finger against the badge stuck to the front of his suit.

'So you saw her last night,' said Greta, glad to be finally getting somewhere. 'Who else was there? Was anyone acting suspiciously?'

She was thinking, but not saying, *Maybe Aunt Tabitha's been kidnapped. But why?*

'Spoke to many. "Hello, hello," she said.

"Dining hall that way, bedrooms that way," she said. "Swimming pool downstairs,"* she said. A human person asked where land dugong should stay. She had made no arrangements. They argued. No special land dugong room. Blah blah blah. I left. Heard no more.'

'This human,' Greta asked. 'What did he or she look like?'

'He or she has face like a human. Round pupils. Smelling lump. Many small interior beaks in mouth-hole. He or she has four bony un-tentacles.'

This wasn't much help. Greta understood that Ticklenesser was trying his best, but it was clear all humans looked pretty much the same to him. That must be why Aunt Tabitha had handed out name badges.

* The swimming pool had been filled with salt water so that Ticklenesser had somewhere to relax outside his reverse diving suit. Aunt Tabitha was thoughtful like that.

She had to find a man or woman who had been looking for a place to keep his or her land dugong. If he or she had been arguing with Aunt Tabitha, then Greta had some hard questions to ask him or her.

One of which was: *What have you done to my aunt?*

Another of which was: *What's a land dugong?*

As she left the room, Ticklenesser turned back to the cabinet he'd been examining when Greta had arrived, pressing buttons and making nothing happen. It looked to Greta's eyes like he couldn't get his invention to work, assuming that the cabinet was his. She wanted to ask him about it – asking questions about things was what she did – but the question of her aunt's whereabouts was much more important right now.

So she left the octopus fiddling with the switches and the flashing lights that didn't flash (or come on at all) and walked deeper into the Hester Sometimes Conference Centre and Immobile Library, in search of the truth (and her aunt.) (And the person with the land dugong.)*

* If Greta had only asked the octopus about his invention at this point in the investigation she might've saved herself a whole lot of time. However, she didn't, and it's because she didn't that the world was saved from the endless appetite of the unstoppable amoeba monsters. So it's swings and roundabouts, you could say.

CHAPTER SIX

Brigadier Ryefoot-fforwerd (Rtd)'s Back Garden, Upper Lowerbridge, England, Earth

LAST SATURDAY (MID-MORNING)

'COOEE?' CALLED PC DELINQUENT, Upper Lowerbridge's only policeman, as he stood on tiptoe and peered over Brigadier Ryefoot-fforwerd (Rtd)'s back gate.

Two large, wobbly shapes wobbled on the Brigadier's lawn.

Neither of them answered the officer's question.

PC Delinquent could just make out the Brigadier waving at him from behind the big transparent wobbly shape on the left.

'Are you all right, Brigadier?' he called.

There was no answer.

Feeling the situation to be urgent, if confusing, the policeman used all of his wit* to climb down from his tiptoes and open the Brigadier's gate. He then entered the garden, ready to speak to the elderly military man face to face. (He had put his earplugs in when he'd got off his bike at the edge of the pavement, because it was well known that a conversation with the Brigadier was always conducted at full volume,

* About two hundred and fifty millivits. Not enough to do three things at once, but more than enough to give directions to the church hall from just outside the church hall.

58

since the old man was, what is politely called, LOUD.)

As he walked up the path, PC Delinquent saw that, in fact, the Brigadier was not stood *behind* the blob on the left, waving at him *through* it, as he'd thought. The Brigadier was actually *inside* the large jelly-like shape, slowly being dissolved and digested, and it was only the bounciness of the great wobbly blob that had made it look like the old man was waving.

PC Delinquent couldn't help but have a little chuckle at his mistake. He was always doing things like that, his mum said. She wouldn't half laugh at this one when he went round to see her on Sunday for dinner.*

'PC Delinquent!' shouted a voice from above. 'Look out!'

* She insisted that he come home for a Sunday roast every week, even if it meant his wife got upset since she wasn't invited and had to watch through the window, while eating her packed lunch.

PC Delinquent didn't look up in surprise at the unexpected advice, since his earplugs caused him to hear nothing.

He looked down instead.

Something had touched his leg.

A fat, pulsating, transparent, jelly-like blob was encircling his knee. It was attached to the fat, pulsating, transparent, jelly-like blob that wobbled next to the one in which the remains of the Brigadier floated.

He tried to run, but he was stuck.

He pulled his truncheon out and hit the blob.

He tried to run again.

Still stuck.

Nothing helped.

He was slowly engulfed by more and more of the jelly-like blob.

'Help!' he shouted. 'Help me!'

But within a minute he was silent and staring out at the world from inside a wobbling amoeba monster.

In the upstairs window of the house whose garden backed on to the Brigadier's garden,

Mr Jamali turned to his wife and said, 'I tried to warn him.'

'You did, dear,' she said. 'That you did.'

'If only he'd run quicker …'

'Maybe,' she said.

'Or if only he'd stayed further away …'

'Maybe,' she said.

'Oh dear,' he said.

They stood in silence for a bit, passing the binoculars back and forth, watching the policeman being slowly digested, until the clock chimed half past eleven and they had to go out to play rounders with the Cohens and Fluke Godwinson's cousin Ralph, who was visiting that weekend from East Westerton.

By the time they'd put on their shoes* and gone to the park and thrown the first ball, the fates of PC Delinquent and the

*They were in the boot of the car, which was at the garage in Lower Upperbridge being mended.

Brigadier had completely slipped their minds.

And while the Jamalis enjoyed their ball game in the bright autumnal sunshine that had quite washed away the greyness of the morning, Greta's garden continued to fill with the jelly-like creatures.

They flopped, one by one, over the lip of the great deep hole, dodging the occasional visit from the automatic spade that continued to dig ever deeper towards the centre of the Earth.

They sat basking in the sunshine before wobbling off, hunger driving their brainless cells to search for food.

Food.

Food!

CHAPTER SEVEN

Hester Sometimes Conference Centre and Immobile Library, Near Upper Lowerbridge, England, Earth

LAST SATURDAY (MID-MORNING)

IN FRONT OF a large set of double doors, above which were printed the words *MAIN HALL*, were a trio of scientists.

They all looked the same, identical like photocopies or triplets, and according to the name badges that Greta read, they went by the names of Bellerophon Alpha, Bellerophon Beta and Bellerophon 3.

They were staring at the doors and talking amongst themselves.

'But we don't have the key,' said Bellerophon Alpha.

'You've said that already,' said Bellerophon Beta.

'But imagine if we did,' said Bellerophon 3. 'We'd be able to uncancel the Twelfth Annual Festival of New Stuff (TAFoNS, for short). We'd be heroes!'

'You keep out of this,' said Bellerophon Alpha.

'Yeah, keep your big nose out,' said Bellerophon Beta.

'But it's exactly the same size as your nose,' objected Bellerophon 3.

'What did you say?' said Bellerophon Beta, threateningly waving a clenched fist close to Bellerophon 3's nose.

'Actually, he's right,' said Bellerophon Alpha to Bellerophon Beta.

'I don't care if he's right or not,' said Bellerophon Beta, 'he shouldn't get involved. It's none of his business.'

'Excuse me. I'm stood right here,' said Bellerophon 3, waving and looking close to tears.

'I don't care where you're stood, you idiot,' said Bellerophon Beta. 'You're always in the flipping way.'

'If *I'm* an idiot,' said Bellerophon 3, out of the corner of his mouth, 'what does that make you?'

Bellerophon Beta gave a huff and turned his back on the other two, and suddenly saw Greta stood there watching.

'Oh,' he said, flustered and replacing his angry red face with an embarrassed red face. 'I'm sorry, I didn't know you were there.'

Bellerophon Beta gave Greta a sharp bow and stalked off, sweeping past her and out of the room.

The other two Bellerophons turned and saw Greta and immediately switched on bright and identical fake smiles.

'Was it something I said?' said Greta, who hadn't said anything yet, and so, quite rightly, assumed the answer to her question to be 'No'.

'No,' said Bellerophon 3, confirming her assumption.

'Oh, don't mind Beta,' said Bellerophon Alpha, 'he's just overtired. You know how he gets.'

Greta didn't mention that she didn't know how he got, having never met any of them before, but just said, 'I'm looking for my aunt.'

'Aunt Tabitha?' asked Bellerophon 3.

'Yes, that's the aunt,' said Greta. 'Have you seen her?'

'No, not today,' said Bellerophon Alpha. 'Word is she's gone missing, with the keys to the main hall. I don't suppose she gave you the spare keys? If we can't get into the main hall, we can't do our presentations, and if we can't do those we won't be able to vote for the Best in Show and no one will get the Big Golden Rosette of Science and Technology. It's a bit of a nightmare.'

'Yes,' said Bellerophon 3. 'Quite so. If she'd planned on going off for the weekend, the least she could've done was leave the keys with someone responsible. I remember the Seventh Annual Festival of New Stuff (SAFoNS, for short), when Jemima Postcard was tragically killed in that inflatable sherbet accident. She'd left the spare keys with Ivor Cathedral and he was able to open up the next morning, so everything was fine.'

'You weren't there,' said Bellerophon Alpha coldly, turning on Bellerophon 3 with a glower. 'It was just me and Beta back then. You don't remember it. I can see why he gets so miffed with you, 3. Saying things like that all the time.'

'But –' said Bellerophon 3.

'Oh! I don't have time for this. I've got to go calm Beta down *and* feed the miniature ostriches.'

Before Greta had time to say 'Miniature ostriches?', Bellerophon Alpha strode off, head in the air and the scent of dismissal wafting behind him.

Then she said, 'Miniature ostriches?'

Bellerophon 3 watched his lookalike leave and then turned to Greta.

'Yes,' he said. 'We've managed to create miniature ostriches. They lay eggs the same size as chicken eggs, which means you no longer have to spend hours boiling them; you can do it in minutes. We think it'll save people a lot of time.'

Then he said, 'Oh, why do I always do it?'

'Do what?' Greta asked, in her most soft and understanding voice.*

'Put my foot in it,' Bellerophon 3 said glumly.

'Ah,' said Greta. 'Did you have an accident with Mr Buffalo's cow? I might have some tissues if you need to clean your shoe … Hang on …'

She patted her pockets.

Bellerophon 3 laughed a small but genuine laugh, before looking sad again.

* This was a basic skill quickly mastered by even the most junior reporter: pretend to be interested and sympathetic. Do that, and pretty soon the person you're talking to will spill some damn fine beans right in your lap (or, even better, in your notebook).

74

'No, that's not what I meant,' he said. 'It's them two. I can't ever seem to say the right thing to them.'

'Are you all brothers?' asked Greta. 'Triplets?'

'No, not exactly. *They're* brothers,' said Bellerophon 3. 'Twins … But I'm a clone. They grew me in a jar in the shed. I was born three weeks ago.'

'Oh,' said Greta. 'That's interesting.' (It wasn't, and she was thinking about her aunt, how she made things in her shed and where she might be now. At some point

Greta would have to go round Aunt Tabitha's house, just to make sure she hadn't gone home for some reason. Maybe she'd had a bump on the head and got amnesia.)

'The problem is,' Bellerophon 3 was going on, not having noticed Greta's lack of interest (she kept her face smiling and nodding, like a good interviewer does), 'I was born with all the memories and knowledge of Bellerophon Alpha and Bellerophon Beta. Everything it took them years and years to learn, everything they had studied for their whole lifetimes … it was all already in my brain when I was decanted.'

'Oh,' said Greta, finally hearing something useful, 'do you know what a land dugong is, then?'

'I'm sorry?'

'A land dugong. Mr Ticklenesser mentioned it, and I think it's a clue.'

'A land dugong? No. I'm sorry, I don't. I'm pretty sure it's not a flightless African bird. I know all of those,' said Bellerophon 3. Then he started talking about himself again. 'And so,' he said, 'you see, that's why they resent me so much. Because they had to work hard and I had it easy.' He sounded close to tears. 'But they're the ones who made me like that, so I don't really —'

'My aunt,' interrupted Greta, not wanting to see a clone man cry. 'Tell me when you last saw my aunt.'

'Oh. Um,' he said with a sniff and a pulling-himself-together nod. 'I suppose it was after dinner last night. I was going up to our room with Alpha and Beta, and we passed Aunt Tabitha in the entrance hall – you know, at the front.'

Greta nodded.

'She was talking to a woman with a little grey beard and a vacuum cleaner. She said, "Just do around the skirting boards and give the corridors a quick going over, and that will do for this evening. I'm going to give my new thing one last test run." And then, this morning, no one could find her, or her keys, and Mr Buffalo took charge and borrowed my scruffy black pen and wrote 'Cancelled' on the sign, so that any scientists arriving today wouldn't waste their time coming inside … and,' he said, patting his pockets, 'I've not seen that scruffy black pen since.'

Greta added things up in her head. The picture of her aunt's movements was becoming clearer. The evening before, after greeting all the scientists and inventors, she'd argued with someone about where their land dugong should stay, then everybody had eaten dinner, and she'd told Mrs Hummock* that she was going to test her new invention.* And then … Aunt Tabitha was never seen again, along with Bellerophon 3's scruffy black pen, although she had a pretty good idea where that was, having seen Mr Buffalo pat his scruffy black pen-shaped pocket earlier.

Since she was having no luck finding the person with the land dugong, Greta probably ought to go back into town to have a word with Mrs Hummock and visit Aunt Tabitha's house. Follow the new clues! And even if she didn't find her aunt in her Inventing Shed, maybe she could learn what

* Mrs Hummock was the only lady in Upper Lowerbridge who had a little grey beard (Fluke Godwinson's was luxurious and golden). So she was working up at the Hester Sometimes Conference Centre and Immobile Library as a cleaner? That was new news to Greta.

★ Aunt Tabitha hadn't told Greta what she was working on, so Greta didn't know what to look for. Was it in Aunt Tabitha's shed or was it already at the Hester Sometimes Conference Centre and Immobile Library? Greta would probably only find out when she found her aunt, and vice versa.

her new invention was. Either way it would be useful.

But still, that land dugong nagged at her mind …

CHAPTER EIGHT

Jessica Plumb's House, Upper Lowerbridge, England, Earth

LAST SATURDAY (LUNCHTIME)

JESSICA PLUMB RAN downstairs and answered the telephone.

It had been ringing and no one else was answering it.

Her dad was off in a world of his own (or, more accurately, was off in the front room) doing his snoring-yoga, and her mum was in the shopping centre in Inner Nobridge dressed as a crocodile and handing out free samples of toothpaste.

Jessica had been lying on her bed, reading a book called *Most Ladies Like Murder*, about a pair of girls at boarding school who devise ever more ingenious methods of doing away with unpleasant teachers. She liked these books, mainly because the two girls used science to do their murders,* and Jessica loved reading about science.

Down in the hallway, the little table beside the long mirror was rattling as the telephone on top of it rang violently.

'Upper Lowerbridge, seven, three, eight, four, nine, oh, five, six, two, five, two, eight, four, nine, five, double eight, seven, three, oh, nine, two, six,' she said brightly.

That wasn't actually the phone number,

* For example, the first teacher to die, Miss Bagpipe, was 'accidentally' electrocuted to death when the new hat she was wearing turned out to conceal a concealed lightning rod. (The hat had been a present from a 'mysterious benefactor'.)

82

but she always enjoyed the moment of quiet at the other end as the person phoning the house thought, *Oh, maybe I've got the wrong number.*

There was no silence this time, however. Even before she'd finished rattling off random numbers, the voice at the other end had begun talking over her.

'Jessica. Can you tell me everything you know about land dugongs?'

It was Greta.

'Land dugongs?' asked Jessica.

'Yes. I don't know what they are, but I thought you might know. You watch those sorts of programmes on the television.'

'Well,' said Jessica, thinking. 'A dugong is another name for a manatee. I think it might be a subspecies. David Volelove talked about them in episode seven of *All the Animals of Earth, Alphabetically*, series seventeen.'

'Ah,' said Greta, who'd given up watching it at the end of series one (at 'antelope, common').

'A manatee,' Jessica went on, 'is also called a sea cow. I think it's because they're big and slow and just sort of graze on sea vegetation, a bit like a cow grazes on land grasses.'

'Aha!' said Greta down the phone. (Jessica could tell from the tone of the 'Aha!' that her

84

friend had raised a finger in the air in triumph as she'd said it.) 'That means a land dugong is actually a land manatee, which is a land sea cow, which is just an ordinary cow.  Brilliant. I wonder if he's already caught his rocket? I need to have a word with that chap.'

'What chap?' asked Jessica. It sounded like her pal was having an adventure, probably being an ace newspaper reporter.

'A man with a cow,' Greta said. 'He's called Buffalo.'

'Walbur P. Buffalo?' said Jessica. 'I've

read about him. He's an inventor from Wyoming. He's forty-seven years old and his hobbies include ice-cream making, eye-patch customising and moustaches.'

'Interesting,' said Greta.

'He's in this year's *Big Book of Inventors to Watch*. He's on page thirty, opposite Amanda Crosshatch, who is your Aunt Tabitha's nemesis. They've been rivals, her and Crosshatch, ever since they both invented the automatic daffodil. It was just a coincidence, but they only found out when they both presented it at the Fourth Annual Festival of New Stuff (FAFoNS, for short). Ever since then … it's been …'

There was silence on the end of the phone for a moment.

Jessica wondered if Greta was still there. She knew that sometimes Greta would go before Jessica had finished a long sentence, if, for example, she needed to be somewhere urgently. It wasn't bad manners, it was just the way Greta was: she didn't have time for faffing about.

But then a voice on the phone said, 'She's missing.'

'Amanda Crosshatch?' asked Jessica. 'She wasn't coming this year. Your Aunt Tabitha told me that she was besieged by giant tortoises and had sent her apologies.'

'No, not Crosshatch,' said Greta (mentally crossing her off the list of suspects for a crime that might not even be a crime, before her name had even been added properly). 'Aunt Tabitha. She's gone missing and I'm looking for her.'

'Oh no,' said Jessica. She was supposed to be helping Aunt Tabitha on Sunday morning. She was going to watch the final presentations and count the votes. She was very excited about it.

'I've got some investigating to do here,' Greta said, 'but then I'll be coming back. I'm going to have to check out Aunt Tabitha's place.'

'I can go do that,' said Jessica. 'I'll sneak out and meet you over there. See you soon.'

'OK.'

There was a click and then the line went dead.

Jessica ran upstairs to get the spare key for Aunt Tabitha's Inventing Shed out of her Secret Drawer of Aunt Tabitha-Related Stuff.

She thought Aunt Tabitha was amazing. Meeting her and Greta were the best things that had ever happened to her. Not everyone was lucky enough to have a best friend with an aunt who was a brilliant inventor.

When she'd been eight years old, Jessica had expected her life to be just the usual thing an eight-year-old kid expects their life to be: schoolwork and homework and growing up into the sort of person who dresses up as a crocodile in the local shopping centre in order to persuade passers-by to try a new flavour of toothpaste: *Minty gazelle — smile like a crocodile!*

But then, when she was eight and a half, her parents had moved house (and she had gone with them*). She'd ended up two doors down from Greta and her life had become much more interesting.

She'd seen Greta in the street and had said, 'Hello, my name's Jessica Plumb. What's yours?' and Greta had looked at her

* She was offered the choice of moving with them or staying with the new people moving in, but since they were a family of strict cannibals from Inner Outerbridge, she decided to stick with her mum and dad.

as if it were a bizarre question before eventually saying, 'Greta Zargo,' and they'd been best friends ever since.

When Jessica had met Greta's Aunt Tabitha she'd been dead surprised. She'd never met an inventor before, or anyone who wore goggles outside of the swimming pool or who had been to the Isle of Wight. She had never dreamt that you could be or do such things. Her mum and dad weren't inventors; they were just ordinary people who wore crocodile costumes in shopping centres.

Greta and Aunt Tabitha had opened doors in Jessica's future.

Once, when Greta was off investigating something or other,* Jessica had been allowed to sit in Aunt Tabitha's Inventing Shed as the woman built a pair of socks that

* Greta had asked: 'Jessica, how many fish can a cat eat before it's sick?' and had got on her bike as soon as Jessica had answered: 'Depends on how big the fish are.' That was all Jessica ever knew of that particular investigation.

changed colour when the person wearing them fell a distance of at least three steps on an average staircase. Aunt Tabitha said that if she could get them to change colour *before* the person wearing them fell a distance of at least three steps on an average staircase, then they would be a really useful addition to the world of Early Warning Clothing.*

Jessica had grinned from ear to over there as she'd watched, and, although Aunt Tabitha had never got the socks to work *exactly* as she'd hoped, Jessica still wore them on special occasions. And, because she was careful, they had *never* changed colour. Not even *once*.

She was wearing ordinary socks now though, and she was worried. Not about the socks, but about Aunt Tabitha. If such a

* Alongside, for example, the Pullover Pullover, which detects when a driver is about to fall asleep and prods them with electric shocks until they stop the car, and Smittens, which heat up in the presence of fanciable people (also, in some regions, sold as 'gloves').

brilliant woman was missing, what hope was there for the rest of us?

She whispered, 'Dad, I'm popping out for a bit,' because she didn't want to wake him in the middle of his snoring-yoga, and then she slipped through the kitchen and pulled open the back door.

Her bike was in the bike shed, which was in the garden, and cycling was the quickest way to get over the road to Aunt Tabitha's house, and she was in a hurry.

Unfortunately, she was in so much of a hurry, and her mind was so filled with worry for Aunt Tabitha, that she didn't notice the large blob-shaped thing on the patio and ran straight into it.

It was oddly warm, dry and sticky, like falling face first on to a duvet made of adhesive marshmallow.

Struggle as she could, and as she did, it was a matter of mere moments before Jessica was inside the amoeba monster, engulfed, swallowed and stuck.

The last thing she thought was a rather disappointing, *Uh-oh*.

CHAPTER NINE

Hester Sometimes Conference Centre and Immobile Library, Near Upper Lowerbridge, England, Earth

LAST SATURDAY (LUNCHTIME)

GRETA PUT THE phone down and picked up her notepad.

Knowing that Jessica was on the case as well was a good thing. It meant there was no need for her to *rush* back to town, back to

Aunt Tabitha's house, not straight away. Jessica would soon be there and if, for some reason, Aunt Tabitha was simply stuck in her Inventing Shed (maybe she'd turned the door handle invisible or something), then Jessica could set her free.

In the meantime, Greta could go looking for Walbur P. Buffalo and his 'land dugong' on the off-chance they'd not actually left yet.* And then she'd go talk to Mrs Hummock. They were her two key people-of-interest in this investigation (them and Aunt Tabitha, of course).

She had found the telephone in the Immobile Library. The Immobile Library was a small van full of books, parked in a courtyard right in the middle of the grand house that made up the Hester Sometimes Conference Centre.★

* They weren't going to walk all the way to the rocket-port, were they? Which meant they might still be waiting for a taxi.

★ Hester Sometimes had famously parked her Mobile Library late one night in a thunderstorm, thirty-odd years ago. In the morning she discovered she'd somehow parked the van in the courtyard, and it was impossible to get it out without knocking down a section of the manor house, and so the Mobile Library became the Immobile Library that it still was.

As Greta set the glass dome back over the phone she heard a voice behind her say, 'And who are you? And what would you like to borrow?'

When she turned round she found herself face to bosom with an elderly lady with short hair, tweed skirts and a small ostrich under one arm.

'Hester Sometimes,' said Greta, a little surprised since the owner of the Hester Sometimes Conference Centre and Immobile Library was supposed to be dead. 'Aren't you supposed to be dead?'

'Not at weekends,' the elderly woman said.

'Oh,' said Greta. She made a note of the answer in her notebook, then she said, 'I don't suppose you've seen my aunt, Aunt Tabitha?'

'Aunt Tabitha? What sort of a name is that? When I was a girl, only cats and servants were called Tabitha, and only aunts were called Aunt. It's a rum old world all turned topsy-turvy, but what can you do? I mean, just look at this ...' Hester Sometimes held the small ostrich up, its long legs dangling in the air either side of her hand.

'When I was a girl, these things were the size of ... oh, I don't know ... the size of ostriches ... but now look at them. Tiny little things. And chocolate bars have got smaller too. But the prices keep going up.' She shook her head. 'Now, what was it you wanted to borrow?'

'I'm afraid I don't want to borrow anything,' said Greta. 'I was just using the telephone as part of an investigation I'm undertaking to discover the whereabouts of my missing aunt.'

Hester Sometimes put the ostrich on a shelf and pulled a book from a different shelf. 'This might help,' she said, handing it to Greta and winking.

'What is it?' Greta asked.

Hester Sometimes looked at her for a moment, and then said, 'It's a book.'

Greta looked back.

The woman was being silly, and Greta didn't approve of silly.

They exchanged a long look, neither of them willing to break eye contact first.

The stalemate was finally interrupted by the ostrich quietly laying an egg about the size of a hen's egg, which rolled slowly off the shelf and fell to the floor with a *splatch!*

Hester and Greta turned to look at the ostrich, the egg and the floor in turn, and then looked at each other again.

Their stare went on for a few seconds longer, then Hester Sometimes said, 'Push off now, will you? I've got some cleaning up to do. Shoo!'

Greta didn't argue. She didn't see herself getting any help from the old lady, and so she climbed out of the Immobile Library, down the steps and into the chill fresh air of the early afternoon.

OK, she thought, taking a deep breath, *let's go find Walbur P. Buffalo and his land dugong, Simon, and ask them some tough questions. Aunt Tabitha's disappearance has a bottom and I want to get to it, because if she's anywhere, she's going to be there.*

And with that, she walked from the

courtyard into a corridor and from there to another corridor, and, as expected, not seeing Buffalo anywhere inside, from there she made her way through the entrance hall and out on to the front drive, where her bicycle still lay on the gravel.

Just before she pulled her bike upright and began to pedal off down the drive in the direction she'd last seen the man and his cow heading, she looked at the book Hester Sometimes had lent her, which was still in her bicycle-bell-ringing hand.

She suddenly remembered the wink Hester Sometimes had given her with the book, and, combining that with the fact that the old lady was *sometimes dead*, wondered if she'd actually been given the book as some sort of occult clue from *the other side*.

A Girl's Guide to Mars, it said on the front cover.

Oh well, thought Greta, slightly disappointed but not entirely surprised.* She tucked the pocket-sized book into her jacket pocket. *I'd best keep it safe for the old lady.*

And then she began the long, uphill cycle along the drive, towards where she hoped Buffalo was still waiting for his taxi.*

* If there was one place she could rule out Aunt Tabitha having disappeared to it was obviously Mars.

★ It might seem an odd hope to have, it being quite a while since Buffalo had left, but Greta knew two important facts: firstly, very few taxis in the Upper Loverbridge area were adapted to carry cows; and secondly, taxis weren't allowed to stop within five hundred metres of the Hester Sometimes Conference Centre and Immobile Library, because of low-flying flying fish.

CHAPTER TEN

Mr Teachbaddly's House, Upper Lowerbridge, England, Earth

LAST SATURDAY (EARLY AFTERNOON)

THERE WAS A ring at the doorbell. Oscar Teachbaddly stumbled downstairs, damp hair flapping and slippers squelching on his feet.

He'd just been heading into the seventh hour of his first Long Bath* of the school ⟶

* A 'Long Bath' can be differentiated from a 'long bath' not only by the length of time involved but also by the range of food, drink and reading material taken into the bathroom with the bather. Generally speaking: one round of toasted cheese sandwiches, a cup of tea and a copy of this month's Teach That! suggests a long bath; a picnic hamper, a minibar full of fizzy pop and a boxed set of Augusta Crispy novels suggest a Long Bath.

holidays and he wasn't happy about being dragged out of it.

The doorbell rang again as he reached the front hall and double-checked that his towel was tightly wound around him.

His housemates, Julian and Barry and Simon and Clive and Petros and Aaron and Sebastian and Esteban and Andrew and Big Derek and Sarah and Little Derek and Ivan and Sandra, had gone out for the day to see an exhibition about herring fishermen in seventeenth-century Finland, at the Lower Upperbridge Museum of Herring. Mr Teachbaddly hadn't heard them come back yet, and was assuming that this was them ringing the bell because they'd forgotten their key.

It wouldn't be the first time.

They had invited him to the museum

with them, of course, but, since it was the first day of the school holidays (or 'freedom' as he called it), and since it was an exhibition about herring fishermen in seventeenth-century Finland, he hadn't gone. Herring always brought him out in a rash, made his breath smell all sort-of herring-y and reminded him of that bad herring experience he'd had as a small boy.

He felt a little *itchy* just thinking about it, and that, combined with the annoyance of them not having their key yet again, made him feel particularly short-tempered.

'How many times do I have to tell you –' he began as he pulled the front door open and was immediately engulfed in the surging wave of transparent jelly that flooded into the hallway.

The last things he saw were the floating faces of Julian and Barry and Simon and Clive and Petros and Aaron and Sebastian and Esteban and Andrew and Big Derek and Sarah and Little Derek and Ivan and Sandra, deep inside the amoeba monster that had swallowed them two minutes earlier, as they stood in the front garden rummaging through their pockets for their front door key.

The key glinted teasingly in Little Derek's hand as Mr Teachbaddly was slowly absorbed and digested by the jiggling transparent jelly.

In the last hour or so, a few amoeba monsters had wandered out from the row of gardens between the houses and into the street.

More were heading that way, hampered only by their slow, wobbling, slithering walk. They were hungry and driven by mindless instinct towards things they could eat.

The jelly-like blobs that had already found food sat still, in place, slowly digesting their meals.

Small amoeba monsters wobbled, digesting birds and puppies and squirrels. (Even the hedgehog who'd woken up specially for the Brigadier's yawn hadn't been safe. She'd rolled herself up and had been as prickly as she could, but her tiny spikes hadn't even made the amoeba monster pause.)

Larger monsters had swallowed other residents of the town, who'd been unlucky enough to find themselves in the way of a slow-moving giant blob of jelly:

Sophie Doodad, who ran the corner shop, had been gardening (Saturday being half-day opening) when she was eaten.

Little Gwendoline Boredom and her brother, Bogof, had been playing cowgirls and astronauts on the patio when they were eaten.

Rudyard Ampofo had made some toast for his lunch and was surprised to see the face of Bobby Butterside, a woman who presented the weather on the local TV, appear in the burn marks. He had been on the phone to the TV station to lodge a formal complaint when he was eaten.

And so the day went on.

The creatures advanced their slow, ceaseless doom.

They were slow, oh yes, but they were also proving to be remarkably unstoppable. One had lumbered over the upturned prongs of a rake without being punctured; another had swallowed a flaming barbecue without being burnt; and one had been cut in half by a falling chainsaw, leaving two slightly smaller amoeba monsters wobbling off in different directions. They were, it seemed, quite indestructible.

And so it went.

They wobbled.

Threateningly.

Menacingly.

Jellyly.

In time, the whole Earth, and everything on it, would be theirs for the eating.

CHAPTER ELEVEN

Just outside the Hester Sometimes Conference Centre and Immobile Library, Near Upper Lowerbridge, England, Earth

LAST SATURDAY (EARLY AFTERNOON)

'**I HEAR YOU** had an argument with my aunt,' said Greta, skidding to a stop on her bike.

She'd just reached the end of the Hester

Sometimes Conference Centre and Immobile Library's long drive, where it met the road from Upper Lowerbridge to Middling Otherbridge.

In front of her, on the corner, was Walbur P. Buffalo and his white-coloured, brown-coloured cow, Simon.

Buffalo was sitting on a suitcase and Simon was standing on the grass verge.

The man looked miserable and frustrated and the cow looked like a cow.

They were, as Greta had been right to hope, still waiting for a taxi to take them to the rocket-port.

'What are you talking about?' he said, looking up. He was still using, Greta noticed, the accent he'd been using before.

'I have a reliable witness,' she said, 'who has reported a heated disagreement between you and my aunt last night. Do you want to tell me about it?'

'Your aunt? Oh, you mean the lady who's supposed to be running this duck shoot?'

Duck shoot? thought Greta. *What's he on about?*

'Yeah, sure,' Mr Buffalo went on, without answering Greta's thoughts, which he hadn't heard, since he'd invented a cow who 'served' burgers, not a telepathic pair of sunglasses. 'The old girl and I exchanged a few words. She hadn't fixed up a room for Simon here.' He patted the cow, who mooed softly. 'Even though I ticked the right box on the booking form. She said I hadn't and I said I had and she said I hadn't ... And then, after a bit of back and forth, she changed my room to one on the ground floor, and Simon

117

was able to sleep over with me. Argument finished.'

'Mmm,' said Greta. 'Are you sure the argument was over? You didn't sneak out later and do something untoward that resulted in my aunt going missing? Because you were ... *angry*?'

'I wasn't ... *angry*,' Mr Buffalo said. 'Once it got sorted I was ... *happy*. Simon gets scared sleeping on her own in new places, so it worked out fine having her in with me. Better than if she'd had her own room, even.'

Greta tapped her pencil on her notepad. His story sounded plausible.

'So,' she said, 'after you got your room changed, what happened then? When did you last see Aunt Tabitha?'

'Well, I skipped dinner. I had a burger in

my room. But I think most everybody else had some big caboodle in the dining hall. Simon don't much care for that sort of thing, so we had an early night. But ...'

He paused.

'But what?'

'But we was woken up about ... eleven o'clock ... by a vacuum cleaner. It was crazy. Who'd be cleaning at that time of night?'

'Mrs Hummock,' said Greta, nodding knowingly. And that was why she was next on Greta's list.

'Oh, it's you,' said Mrs Hummock.

'Yes, it's me,' said Greta.

They had met before and didn't get on very well, because of *things*.

'Well?'

'Mrs Hummock,' said Greta, 'when did you last see my aunt?'

'She's *your* aunt,' said Mrs Hummock. 'When did *you* last see her?'

'I asked first,' said Greta.

Mrs Hummock huffed, stroked her little grey beard and said, 'Well, it was last night, if you must know. Very rude she was too. Owes me money.'

'Oh?'

'Had me up to the Hall to do a bit of cleaning. I'm proud to say I've pushed a vacuum cleaner or two in my time. I've got certificates. And a medal. I vacuumed for England once upon a time. I stood there on that podium, like a star, as they all applauded. Best day of my life, that was.'

'You won bronze, didn't you?' asked Greta innocently.

'A medal's still a medal,' snapped Mrs Hummock. 'Anyway, what have you ever won? Eh?'

Greta tapped her pencil on her notepad and said nothing.

'Well,' Mrs Hummock said, after the silence became awkward, 'she calls me up to the big house last night. After dinner this was. The place needed a spruce up before her big science-y shindig this weekend. And so I push the vacuum round, give it all a good going-over. And then, when I was done, she was gone.'

'Gone?'

'Yes. Vanished off into the night. Gone home, I guessed, and me stood there with my hand out, waiting for my agreed remuneration, like a chump. I'll be demanding payment in advance for the next job she asks me to do. That's for sure, and you can tell her that.'

Greta thought about this.

'Did you see anyone else around? Anyone suspicious while you were vacuuming?'

'Anyone suspicious?'

'Yes?'

'Anyone *suspicious*?'

'Yes.'

'*Anyone* suspicious?'

'Ye-e-s?'

'Have you met those idiots your aunt's invited? They're *all* suspicious if you ask me. What do they need to be inventing all these new things for? Don't we have enough *stuff* already?'

'I see,' said Greta. 'So you don't like inventors and scientists? Is that what you're saying, Mrs Hummock? You, the last person to have seen my aunt before she vanished, have a personal dislike of exactly the sort of person my aunt is? Hmm? It sounds awfully suspicious to me.'

'I won't stand for such impertinence on my doorstep,' said Mrs Hummock. 'How dare you suggest I had anything to do with anything? If you make another insinuation like that I'm going to phone Wilf up and have a word in his ear.'*

* Wilf was Wilfred Inglebath, Greta's editor at The Local Newspaper. He was also Mrs Hummock's brother-in-law.

'That doesn't matter any more,' Greta said. 'This is bigger than an award-winning newspaper story. This is my aunt.'

The door slammed in her face with a rattle.

Greta climbed back on her bike and pedalled round the corner and down the street towards Aunt Tabitha's house.

The town seemed very quiet now that Mrs Hummock had stopped talking.

Only the distant *thwock* of a rounders game on the green sounded in the cold, bright air of the afternoon, that and the occasional noise of an odd jellyish wobble, like jelly wobbling somewhere nearby.

Greta leant her bike against the wall of Aunt Tabitha's house and went up the side and into the back garden.

On the lawn sat a wobbling jelly-like thing, about the size of small person, and inside it was a squirrel. A giant squirrel. A giant squirrel called Jonathon.

Why her aunt had encased Jonathon in a sphere of wobbly goo like this was beyond Greta, but she'd long since learnt to accept her aunt's inventions without raising an eyebrow.* Maybe Aunt Tabitha thought a rubberised bouncing squirrel ball was going to be the next big thing in squirrel evolution.* Greta was sure her aunt would tell her, just as soon as she'd been found.

She tried the handle of the Inventing Shed and the door opened.

'Jessica?' she called into the darkness. 'Are you in there? Aunt Tabitha, are *you* there?'

There was no reply.

Greta didn't let the silence worry her. She hadn't expected her aunt to answer, and if her aunt wasn't there then there was no reason for Jessica to be there either. She'd probably popped over, seen that Aunt Tabitha wasn't there and gone home again.

There'd probably be a note waiting for

Greta when she got home, saying, *No sign of Aunt Tabitha in her Inventing Shed. JXP.**

Greta flicked the light on and looked around.

The benches and worktops were covered with all sorts of things that she didn't recognise. Greta didn't have the inventor-y sort of mind, and didn't know the difference between a widget and a wodget and a wadget, which were things that her aunt could tell apart with her eyes closed and through a thick pair of mittens.

Greta didn't know what she was looking for, but she looked for it nonetheless. You never found a clue by not looking.

While she searched, she tried to piece together what she knew:

1. Mr Buffalo had had an argument with Aunt Tabitha, but it was all over when

he had his room changed.

2. The Bellerophons had heard Aunt Tabitha say she had to check her new invention one last time.

3. Mrs Hummock had done the vacuuming.

4. No one had seen Aunt Tabitha since.

So, the missing bit of the story was *the invention*.

Once Greta found out what it was that Aunt Tabitha had been working on, what it was she had gone to check on and, most helpfully perhaps, where she'd been keeping it, then Greta would know where to go next.

(1) Mr Buffalo
(2) The Bellerophons
(3) Mrs Hummock
(4) Where is Aunt Tabitha? What was her invention??

She rummaged across the surfaces, knocking things left and right. She pulled out boxes and looked inside them. She opened cupboards and closed them again quickly, trying to forget what she'd seen. She rummaged in random boxes of even more random bits, bobs and baps* until, eventually ...

'Oh!'

There, pinned up on a corkboard, was a drawing of something Greta had seen before.

It was a blueprint of a cabinet, about the size of a shower cubicle, with the words *Teleport Booth* written neatly below it.

It was the same cabinet that Yevgeny Ticklenesser had been looking at, back at the Hester Sometimes Conference Centre and Immobile Library. So it hadn't been *his* invention, as Greta had assumed, but

* One of the random bits in a box was the missing remote control for the automatic spade that had dug down to where the amoeba monsters had lurked. In her rummaging, Greta accidentally pressed the button labelled 'Self Destruct' and a small, distant, muffled boom! was heard a few seconds later (except she sneezed at the same time and didn't hear it). Greta never knew, but this was the first of two things she would do that would save the world from its almost certain amoeba-monster doom.

Aunt Tabitha's. (Why, then, had he been so interested in it? That was another question she'd be getting an answer to, just as soon as she could return to the Hester Sometimes Conference Centre and Immobile Library and ask it.)

'Aha,' she said.

Everything was falling into place in her brain. She could see what had happened as if she'd been there watching it:

Mr Buffalo, secretly still angry, had pushed Aunt Tabitha into the Teleport Booth and sent her off somewhere;

Or Mr Ticklenesser, upset that the Twelfth Annual Festival of New Stuff (TAFoNS, for short) was going to be better than the Eleventh Annual Festival of New Stuff (EAFoNS, for short) (the one he'd hosted the previous year), had decided to sabotage it by pushing Aunt Tabitha into her Teleport Booth and sending her off somewhere;

Or one of the *original* Bellerophons had decided to frame their clone for a crime he didn't commit by making it look as if he had ruined the Twelfth Annual Festival of New Stuff (TAFoNS, for short) by teleporting Aunt Tabitha away with the keys. Greta bet if she examined the Teleport Booth she'd find one of Bellerophon 3's hairs or fingerprints or lunchboxes;

Or ...

Oh, just because they were the only inventors Greta had spoken to didn't mean, of course, that they were the only ones at the Hester Sometimes Conference Centre and Immobile Library. There were loads more there waiting to show off their inventions – or there had been, before the

Twelfth Annual Festival of New Stuff (TAFoNS, for short) was cancelled. A lot of them, like Mr Buffalo, were probably on their way home already.

Time was short, and the only way Greta could see to solve the mystery was to go and find her aunt and ask her who it was that had sent her away.

As Greta hurried out of the shed, she accidentally knocked over a jar of Know-It-All Brain Food, Aunt Tabitha's experimental brain accelerant, which rolled across the table top, knocking a gas spigot into its 'open' position.

The gas spigot also stopped the jar from rolling any further, so it didn't fall to the floor and smash.* The silence of the bottle not smashing on the shed floor meant Greta did not turn round as she left, and within

133

seconds she was running past the wobbling, partially digested squirrel and back to her bike.

As Greta pedalled speedily past Sophie Doodad's corner shop, a great jelly-like blob monster lunged at her from an alley, but her head was down and her feet were pounding

(she was humming the theme tune from *Now Investigate This!* as she went) and the monstrous amoeba was far too slow.

It wobbled after her for a few metres before giving up and slumphing back towards the middle of town.

CHAPTER TWELVE

A House a Few Streets Away from Greta Zargo's House, Upper Lowerbridge, England, Earth

LAST SATURDAY (LATE AFTERNOON)

THE GAME OF rounders had been so closely fought, and the post-game podcast so enjoyably argumentative, that when Mr and Mrs Jamali finally arrived home they'd completely forgotten the horrors of that morning, when they'd witnessed amoeba monsters eating people in the garden.

Pretty soon Mr Jamali had dinner washed, chopped and in the oven. Then the theme tune to *Celebrities Dropping Antiques* came singing out from the front room and he rushed in to watch it with Mrs Jamali. It was the final, and he was cheering for Hamnet Ovenglove, the World Champion Onion Wrestler,* while Mrs Jamali was waving her pom-poms in support of Rashomon O'Donoghue, the All-England Tiddlyblinks Champion.⋆

When the programme had finished, after a breathless and edge-of-the-seat-ful finale, in which Ovenglove won by three small Roman pots and a Victorian vase to two Japanese netsukes and a painting of a child in old-fashioned trousers, Mr and Mrs Jamali had their dinner.

* *Although he had cried in every match throughout the World Championships, he'd still beaten every onion he'd fought.*

⋆ *Tiddlyblinks is a game exactly like tiddlywinks, except that each player flips two counters at the same time.*

It was only when Mr Jamali opened the back door to throw the scraps out for the terrapins on the patio, that the amoeba monsters came back into his mind.

The reason he was reminded of them just then was that there were seven of them on the patio, wobbling.

Six of them were quite small, beachball-sized or so, and contained the skeletons of the six terrapins who (had previously) roamed their garden.

The seventh was larger and contained nothing but jelly.

With whatever senses the amorphous blob had, it sensed Mr Jamali and plunged forwards towards the doorway.

Mr Jamali slammed the door just in time.

Crash!

'Um,' he called through to the front room, where Mrs Jamali was just settling down to watch *President Slightly's Weekly Address to the Nation*,* 'darling …'

Mr Jamali wasn't sure how to finish the sentence.

The back door rattled behind him.

He turned the key in the lock.

'Darling,' he said, going into the front room. 'I think we should leave.'

'Shhh,' said Mrs Jamali. 'He's just getting to the good bit.'*

'Ooh,' said Mr Jamali as the President said the last few letters, and then he shook his head. 'There's one of those things outside. There's loads of them. I think they want to eat us.'

'What things?'

'Amoeba-y things. You remember. This morning? The Brigadier?'

Crash!

'What's that noise?' asked his wife, looking over his shoulder towards the kitchen.

'It's one of those monsters at the back door. Like I said. We need to go out the front.'

'But we've only just come home.* I was going to have a bath.'

'Maybe have a bath at your sister's? We could go there. I bet there aren't any of

*This wasn't exactly true, but Mr Jamali wasn't in the mood to argue.

these monsters in Lower Upperbridge. Perhaps we can give her a ring on the way?'

'We can't just go out,' Mrs Jamali said.

'Why not?' asked Mr Jamali. 'We're grown ups now, dear. We can go out whenever we want.'

'Well, at least let me have my bath first.'

Crash!

In that crash was also the sound of splintering wood and hinges giving way a bit.

The door was holding for now, but it wouldn't last long.

'No time for that, my sweet,' Mr Jamali said. 'We've got to go now.'

'What *is* that noise? I think someone's trying to break in.'

Mr Jamali sighed.

He hadn't wanted to say this. But …

'They've eaten the terrapins.'

Mrs Jamali's face sank.

'What?'

'The terrapins. These amoeba monsters have eaten them.'

'Gerald Terrapin?'

'Yes.'

'Frances T. Terrapin?'

'Yes.'

'Not, Sir Arthur Conan Terrapin?'

'Yep. All of them. I saw them wobbling inside the jellies.'

'You can't mean Sister Joan Terrapin III?'

'*All* of them. They've *all* been eaten.'

'Terry Terrapin?'

'Yes. Even Terry Terrapin.'

There was a moment's silence broken only by another huge *crash!* from the back door.

'Not, Susan?'

'Susan? Do you mean Susan Bigginthorpe from number twenty-seven? How am I supposed to know if *she's* been eaten by an amoeba monster? Am I supposed to go round and check, knock on her door and say, "Excuse me, Susan, I was wondering if you'd been consumed by a giant blob of jelly? Well have you?".'

'No, not *her*. I meant Susan Terrapin.'

'Oh, yes. *She's* been eaten.'

Mrs Jamali looked thunderstruck.

She rolled up her sleeves, but since she wasn't wearing a long-sleeved top she simply stroked her arms, which felt quite nice but didn't soothe her.

'OK, no one eats my terrapins and gets away with it,' she said.

She pushed Mr Jamali out of the way and strode purposefully into the kitchen.

'All right, you,' she shouted, grabbing an electric whisk off the side and waving it threateningly. 'Let's have at it.'

At that precise moment the back door finally gave way, spraying bits of wood and glass and metal and cat flap all over the kitchen.

The electric whisk whirred and Mrs Jamali plunged it into the gelatinous blob that was splurging towards her.

Tiny bits of jelly sprayed around the kitchen, covering the walls and spattering her face.

'Ha ha!' she shouted. 'I wasn't crowned World Whisk-Fencing Champion of the World for nothing! Look at you die, amoeba monster!'

Unfortunately, as she lunged forward again, pushing the whirring blades even

deeper into the blob, she pulled the plug out of its socket.

The whirring stopped and she found herself stuck, arm-deep inside the wobbling monstrosity.

Mr Jamali tried tugging her. He tried pulling her. He even yanked her, but nothing worked.

He could only watch in horror as Mrs Jamali waved at him from inside the blob.

She was pointing at the kitchen table.

He passed her the book that was sat on the edge. The bookmark showed that she was only a dozen or so pages from the end of *The Dentist Did It*.* If she had to be dissolved and digested by a mindless monster from the middle of the Earth, it seemed a shame not to have something to read while it happened.

* The Dentist Did It was the third book in the Inspector Insight whodunnits-for-people-who-don't-much-like-suspense series of crime novels by Fiona Fibula, following on from For Once It Really Was the Butler and See the Bloke Who's Acting Nervous on Page 37? It Was Him.

The blob had stopped moving, had stopped advancing as soon as it swallowed Mrs Jamali.

It seemed the monster only wanted to eat one meal at a time.

Mr Jamali was safe for the moment.

And so he sat with his wife while she read, until he got bored and went and phoned his sister-in-law to tell her the news.

'I'll be over there as soon as,' she said briskly. 'You hold tight. No fear. No worries.'

She was a field marshall in the army, and if anyone could put a stop to the unstoppable progress of these indestructible amoeba monsters, and beat them once and for all, it was Field Marshall Gwendoline Herbert.

Oh, thought Mr Jamali, *they're going to pay*

for eating Mrs Jamali. They're going to pay big time.

And then, unable to bear watching Mrs Jamali being dissolved and digested any more (it had got to the bit where the bones were beginning to show, which was, quite frankly, disgusting), he went and sat down in the front room and switched on the telly.

After an hour or two of *Cops Solve Swedish Crimes Slowly*, Mr Jamali thought he heard the low rumble of a tank's caterpillar tracks out in the street, and so he got up to go and wave hello at Field Marshall Herbert.*

Help has come at last! he thought.

As he opened the front door, however, the amoeba monster that had been leant against it, enjoying the feel of the cool

* *As it happened, it wasn't the noise of the tank he heard, but that of a piece of his dinner turning sideways in his stomach and setting off a chain reaction of loud grumbles and rumbles.*

painted wood against its outer membrane, collapsed on top of him and engulfed him.

So close, thought Mr Jamali, *so close to safety, and now this. Eaten! And I don't even have anything to read ...*

A few hours earlier, the automatic spade that had dug too deep, freeing these gelatinous horrors from their long, slow slumber in the far pits of the Earth's insides, had received a signal from its long-forgotten controller.

Self destruct! Emergency! Self destruct! Emergency! it had said.

And so the spade, being just a machine made to follow the orders it was given (it had been told *Dig!* once, and it had dug), lit the fuse of its own doom and in a fiery fireball of exploding wood and metal and wires and sheer *spadiness,* it had exploded.

At the time it was on its way up the deep shaft with another shovelful of grit from down below, and it could see the daylight above it.

As it exploded, the walls of the shaft around it collapsed and everything below was buried.

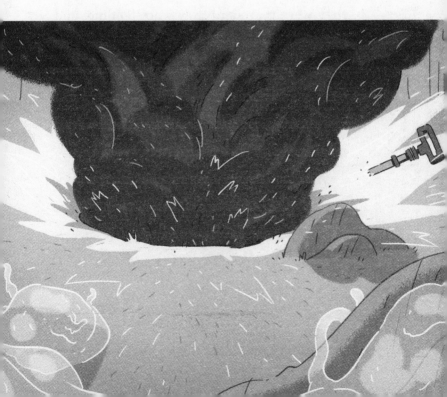

Greta's whole garden slumped, sloping down towards the end with the hole in it, and the jelly-like blob-monsters that were still nearby wobbled.

In their jellyish centres they knew something had changed. They were cut off from their deep, dark homes; they were alone in the upper world, with no more of their kind coming to join them. But still, they were there and they were feeding, and soon they would be splitting, reproducing, multiplying and spreading out further and further in search of more people to eat.*

The world was still theirs for the taking.

And many of them were still hungry.

And the ones that weren't hungry right now would be hungry tomorrow, when even the bones they contained had been

* An amoeba monster is able to split into two new amoeba monsters. (That's how they make babies.) So, maths: before the spade exploded, forty-one monsters had reached the surface. If, on average, they each split in two once per day, then at the end of the first week there would be 2,624 amoeba monsters, at the end of the second week 335,872 monsters and at the end of the third week more than 42 million of them. World domination awaits!.

dissolved and digested, and they were empty once more.

And so they wobbled.

Worryingly.

Fearsomely.

Jellyly.

CHAPTER THIRTEEN

Hester Sometimes Conference Centre and Immobile Library, Near Upper Lowerbridge, England, Earth

LAST SATURDAY (AFTERNOON)

GRETA STOOD IN front of the cabinet that she now knew was Aunt Tabitha's Teleport Booth.

Its flashing lights weren't flashing. They weren't even on.

'I thought it looked important,' said Yevgeny Ticklenesser. 'I have pushed all buttons. Nothing. Nothing happens.'

'Mmm,' said Greta, thinking back to the blueprint she'd seen on her aunt's Inventing Shed wall.

The clicking and whirring of Ticklenesser's reverse diving suit was calming as she tried to remember what the blueprints had shown. It was like the sound of clocks ticking, and Greta liked clocks.

Her parents, who had died accidentally when she was only a baby, had left her several clocks and she took a little time each day to wind them. They all told different times, because none of them worked very well and they all slowed at different rates, and so they were completely pointless as time-keeping devices. But they ticked away, in and out of synch, every day of her life, in the quiet of the house and through the dark of the night. They were like a kindly presence, a soothing 'as long as we're here, everything is all right' sort of backdrop to her life.

And right now, although she was worrying about Aunt Tabitha (about how she thought she'd solved the mystery and would soon be finding her aunt, but had now hit another dead end), that ticking sound kept her away from the edge of panic.

She had found Ticklenesser outside the Hester Sometimes Conference Centre and Immobile Library, right down at the end of the drive. He was in the middle of a gaggle of scientists and inventors who were waiting, just where Walbur P. Buffalo was *still* waiting, for taxis to take them away from the failed Twelfth Annual Festival of New Stuff (TAFoNS, for short).*

* *Walbur P. Buffalo was growing ever angrier as he waited for a cow-friendly taxi to turn up. (One taxi driver had offered to put Simon on the roof rack, but that was just silly, not to mention dangerous.)*

There were all three Bellerophons and Mr Buffalo and Simon, and there was a short, round woman with enormous goggles,* and Yevgeny Ticklenesser in his reverse diving suit, and there were a couple of women with spikey hair and the faint hum of electricity rippling across their faces,✶ and there was a tall man with a beard and dark glasses who knew the names of all the frogs in Denmark.✷

'You lot,' Greta had said, staring at each of them in turn. 'I need you to come with me back to the Hester Sometimes Conference Centre and Immobile Library. I *know* where my aunt is. I'm going to fetch her, and then she'll tell us which one of you it was that tried to get rid of her.'

'What do you mean,' Walbur P. Buffalo

* This was Mildred Mildred, the inventor of the chaotic diary, for people who wanted their life made more interesting.

✶ These were Sparkle and Peach Crumplehorn, the sisters who had invented disposable socks.

✷ This was the famous chef Pierre Doolong, who was meant to be at the Fifth Annual Chef Exhibition (FACE, for short) the following weekend, but who had received a chaotic diary for his birthday, which was, if nothing else, making his life more interesting.

had said, '"which one of you it was that tried to get rid of her"?'

'I think,' Mildred Mildred had said, 'this little girl is accusing us of having nefariously done something to someone. I've never been so insulted in my life.'

'Well, Trout-face,' Bellerophon 3 had said, 'today's your lucky day. Your goggles are stupid-looking and you smell like the inside of an artichoke's handbag. Your inventions are pathetic, except for the Red Butter Knife, which *was* a good invention, but which was curiously similar to the Scarlet Butter Knife we invented the year before. You are also a little bit fat.'

There had been a moment's silence at this outburst, and then Mildred Mildred had pulled herself up to her full height* and said, 'Who are you?' at exactly the same time as

*Which wasn't very high

159

Bellerophon Beta had swung a punch that hit Bellerophon 3 in the arm and knocked him down.

'*You* weren't there!' Bellerophon Beta had shouted. '*I* invented the Scarlet Butter Knife. *Me!* Not *you*. Gah! Stop taking credit for *my* inventions!'

Yevgeny Ticklenesser had whirred and

clicked his way round to where Greta had
stood and said, 'You. Me. I listen. Let us go
together. People here are strange. Let us
leave.'

Greta had nodded and had walked with
the octopus up the driveway, pushing her
bike and leaving the squabbling scientists
behind.

If Aunt Tabitha were to point the finger at one of them as being the one who had tele-ported her away, for whatever 'nefarious'* reason, then it would be up to the police to track them down and throw the book at them. Greta would have loved to have had the police there when the truth was uncovered, and to have got a first-hand report down in her notebook of the way the villain's face went through a series of worried, panicked, proud, startled, happy, confused, creepy, crafty, subdued, sly, shy, innocent, sad, angry, blustering, shattered, sorry, guilty, excited, hungry, flat, orange, fuming, incandescent, found-out and confused (again) expressions, but you don't always get what you want.

Getting her aunt back and having a Big Story for the newspaper would have to be enough.

* It was a Good Word that Mildred Mildred had used and Greta liked to remember Good Words. Clause Twenty in her parents' Last Will and Testament said: Greta, darling, do try to have a nice vocabulary. Don't use the same words all the time. Mix it up a bit. Be a bit thesaurus-ish every now and then.

162

And so Greta and the octopus were back in the Hester Sometimes Conference Centre and Immobile Library, staring at the cabinet her aunt had vanished in.

'These lights,' said Greta, pointing to the bulbs on the cabinet. 'I'm sure they ought to be lit up and flashing. Aunt Tabitha loves putting flashing lights on things. It makes it feel more science-y.'

'But where you keep glowing fishes?'

'Glowing fishes?'

'Yes. In cabinet here, no glowing fish space for flashing lights.'

Greta thought for a moment.

'Do you mean,' she asked, 'that where you come from your flashing lights use glowing fishes to light them?'

'Sometimes glowing plankton, too. Or glowing eels.'

'That's not how it works up here,' she said. 'Here we make lights with electricity.'

'We tried once. Big shock. Now, just glowing fish.'

Of course Ticklenesser didn't use electricity: it's hard to get it underwater. But up here, in the dry of the land, electricity was what everyone used, and it was what the cabinet didn't seem to have any of.

Greta's brain was buzzing now. Things were falling into place like a video of a jigsaw being taken apart played in reverse.

Mrs Hummock!

Greta stepped round to the back of the cabinet and there it was – a plug socket and an unplugged plug.

Mrs Hummock must've unplugged the plug when she plugged her vacuum cleaner in, and then forgotten (perhaps even on purpose?) to plug the Teleport Booth's plug back into the plug socket when she was done.

Greta plugged the plug in.

'Glowing fishes!' said Ticklenesser.

Greta rushed round to the front and – *yes!* – all the lights were on and some of the them *were* flashing.

'Now,' she said triumphantly, 'to go find Aunt Tabitha!'

She stepped into the cabinet and the door slid shut behind her.

There was a big button in the middle of the inside of the door, labelled 'Go!', and a little window through which a slightly taller person would've been able to see the octopus on the outside staring back at them.

'Here goes,' said Greta as she pushed the button.

A sudden gush of freezing air swept around her and she was flash-frozen.

Then three hundred thousand needle-fine ultra-high-power laser beams dismantled her, atom by atom. The exact location of each atom was recorded, as Greta was taken apart, and stored in enormous computer brains that formed the Teleport Booth's upper part.

Soon* Greta had been reduced to a pile of Undifferentiated Atomic Dust, which was swept up by special suction arms and added to the Undifferentiated Atomic Dust already stored in the large Undifferentiated Atomic Dust Vessel underneath the cabinet.

An antennae on the top of the Teleport Booth swivelled round until it found the direction it had been seeking and then began, silently, to transmit a long string of information out into space.

* The process took a little less than ten minutes, but Greta knew nothing of it, having been flash-frozen. Ticklenesser watched in slightly concerned fascination, and took care not to press any of the buttons on the outside of the cabinet, just in case they made the situation worse.

CHAPTER FOURTEEN

The Street Outside Mr and Mrs Jamali's House, Upper Lowerbridge, England, Earth

LAST SATURDAY (EARLY EVENING)

IT WAS GETTING dark by the time Field Marshall Gwendoline Herbert drove her Mark VII Charabang tank into the streets of Upper Lowerbridge.

She swung the large searchlight back and forth as she drove towards her sister's house, catching the glinting, glistening sight of huge jellyish shapes lurching and wobbling in the cold of the evening's air.

They were just like Mr Jamali had described them: giant, blobby, amoeba-ish things filled with floating bones. And there were so many of them around.

So many of *them*, and so few people.

In fact, she could count the number of people she saw on the fingers of one hand.*

It was as if the whole town had been eaten by these obscene creatures.

She stopped her tank a little way up the street from the Jamalis' house and pointed the searchlight that way.

There, on the doorstep, was her brother-in-law, waving at her from inside the gelatinous body of one of the amoeba monsters.

In fact, it was more like the skeleton of her brother-in-law than her brother-in-law himself. Being dissolved and digested had caused him to lose a lot of weight since they'd last met.

Having a well-trained military brain, she knew that a man reduced to a skeleton was not the sort of man you can save. You can't just drag him out of the jelly, give him the

* Specifically her left hand, which had been lost in the Battle of Monsieur Dupont's knee ten years earlier, and had been replaced with an all-purpose Swiss Navy hand, which had many useful things on it, but not what you'd actually call any fingers.

171

kiss of life and expect him to get up and say thank you. He was, what they called in her line of work, 'Beyond-kissing-back-to-life'.

So she pulled the little handles and spun the little wheels and pressed the little buttons that turned the turret of her tank to point its long cannon at the ex-brother-in-law on the doorstep.

The least she could do, if she couldn't kiss him back to life, was avenge his being unfairly and unexpectedly and unkindly digested by a horrible jelly-like monster.

Offering a quick prayer to Krik-Azgodius-Thurible, the God of Tank Commanders, Warriors and Chiropodists, she closed her eyes and pressed the button labelled 'Fire'.

With a loud *BOOM!* a shell flew from the tank's cannon and hurtled, supersonically, straight at the thing on the doorstep.

It was hard to say exactly what happened next, because there was a lot of smoke around to obscure the view, and most of it happened at practically the same time. So, beginning in no particular order, the key points were these:

(a) Field Marshall Gwendoline Herbert thought: *I didn't join the army for fame, but saving the nation from unstoppable amoeba monsters might get me on one of those chat shows the wife watches — maybe* Answer the Question! *or* Let Me Interrupt You! *Oh, that'll make her happy*.

(b) The amoeba monster thought nothing, being mindless and driven only by instinct and being wholly consumed with wholly consuming Mr Jamali, but it did feel a sudden impact which made it wobble tremendously, like a fat man falling off a pogo stick.

(c) The shell that the tank had just fired also thought nothing, being a shell and not a person, but it hit the amoeba monster and bounced off, high into the air, turning tip over tail as it soared up, slowing and slowing until it finally began to fall. And there, below it, if it had had eyes to see (which it didn't), it would have seen the shape of a shed thundering towards it. And then ...

(d) ... another *BOOM!* as the shell smashed through the ceiling of Aunt Tabitha's gas-filled Inventing Shed and exploded.

(e) Clouds of debris and dust and smoke and *stuff* flew high into the air.*

Back over by the tank, the smoke was beginning to clear and Field Marshall Herbert was astonished, and disappointed,

* This was the third part of Greta's two-part solution for saving the world from the invasion of the amoeba monsters, as mentioned earlier. Although Greta knew nothing of it, and was in fact being beamed through space at this moment, it was, nevertheless, down to her that everyone on Earth wasn't eaten. She saved us all. Well done, Greta.

to see the monster she had shot at still sitting on the doorstep, unharmed, unchanged, and wobbling insultingly, with her brother-in-law's bones floating inside it.

'Oh dear,' she said.

Before she was consumed by an amoeba monster herself, which would happen in about eight minutes' time, the Field Marshall tried using a machine gun, a hand grenade and a flame thrower on several different blobs, but none of the weapons left even a mark. Not a single bit of jelly died. It was very annoying.

When they'd spoken on the phone, Mr Jamali had neglected to tell her that these amoeba monster things were indestructible. If she'd known that, she might not have simply rolled over to Upper Lowerbridge in her tank. She might've telephoned High

Command and had them drop a giant dome over the town, or something like that.

Well, she thought, *you live and learn. Except*, she added, *when you only do one of them.*

She had definitely *learnt* something.

And then an amoeba monster searching for food slobbled its way up the side of the tank, and while she was stood in the turret, looking through her binoculars at

something just too far away to see without using binoculars, she was surrounded, swamped and swallowed.

CHAPTER FIFTEEN

Pendragon City, Mars

LAST SATURDAY (EARLY EVENING)

AUNT TABITHA HAD been waiting almost a whole day (and days were over half an hour longer on Mars than they were back on Earth) for the message on the panel on the front of the Teleport Booth to say that the other unit, back on Earth, was working again.

She'd only meant to test it quickly, to make sure it was working properly, ready for her big presentation on Sunday, but somehow something had gone wrong. She didn't know that Mrs Hummock had unplugged the cabinet at the Hester Sometimes Conference Centre and Immobile Library, only that, for some reason, it wasn't receiving.

She had tried phoning Greta to ask her to go and check the Earth-side Teleport Booth, but had stopped trying when she discovered that there wasn't a telephone nearby.

Pendragon City was a small domed city on the surface of the planet Mars. 'City' was, perhaps, something of an exaggeration. It was really just a large transparent dome, waiting for the arrival of the first Marsonauts. There were stacked neatly, boxes of crackers, tins of tinned peaches and bottles of water waiting to be consumed. There were a pair of small robots waiting for new commands. There were boxes that contained deflated transparent domes, waiting to be inflated by the small robots in order to expand the 'City'. And there was Aunt Tabitha's Mars-side Teleport Booth.

That was where she stood.

It was almost a year since she had signed the contract with BASA*, and she'd been brilliant at keeping the secret all this time.

* The British Agency of Space Adventures.

181

Now here she was, the first person to live overnight in Britain's first-ever Martian colony.

The Teleport Booth had been sent to Mars on the spaceship *BSS Arthur*, along with all the supplies and the robots and the dome material. When the spaceship had touched down the robots had trundled out on to Mars's dusty red surface and inflated the dome, filled it with supplies from the spaceship, and plugged the Teleport Booth into the power generator.

Because of this robotic advance mission, the future Martian colonists would now be able to step into the Teleport Booth on Earth, have themselves transmitted through space at the speed of light, and be reassembled on Mars between ten and twenty minutes later. None of that dangerous flying through space in a flimsy tin can for them.

After the first public demonstration of this technology at the Twelfth Annual Festival of New Stuff (TAFoNS, for short), two things were expected to happen. Firstly, the Earth-side Teleport Booth would be moved to BASA headquarters on the Isle of Wight, right next to the cafeteria and just across from the swimming pool, in case the Marsonauts fancied a dip or something nicer to eat than tinned peaches and crackers, and secondly, Amanda Crosshatch would become really jealous when she read about it in *Inventor's Weekly International* (*the* magazine for inventors and inventor enthusiasts).

But it had all gone wrong. Aunt Tabitha had made one final trip through the machine, as she had done several times before, but

183

when she stepped out into the Martian dome she had turned round and seen a worrying message on the display: THIS BOOTH CANNOT FIND THE OTHER BOOTH. TRY AGAIN LATER.

She had lost contact with Earth.

She had hit the Teleport Booth with her hand, a spanner and a tin of peaches, but it didn't seem to help, so then she had sat down and waited.

After an hour or so she had grown bored of waiting.

After another few hours she had grown bored of crackers and peaches and bottled water.

She had put on a spacesuit and gone out the airlock to have a little stroll on the surface, but it was just reddish and stony and not very interesting, since she wasn't a planetary scientist, merely an inventor. There wasn't much you could invent with dust and stones.

So she'd come back in and had another tin of peaches and had sat down, and waited a bit more.

And then, finally, eventually, hours and hours later, it happened: the little light on the panel on the side of the Teleport Booth flicked on and there was a *ding!* noise and the message on the display changed to say: THIS BOOTH HAS FOUND THE OTHER BOOTH.

And without wasting another moment, Aunt Tabitha stepped into the cabinet, let the door hiss shut behind her, pressed the button labelled 'Go!' and was instantly flash-frozen and, shortly thereafter, disassembled by three hundred thousand needle-fine ultra-high-power laser beams

into a pile of Undifferentiated Atomic Dust, with her important information reduced to a long string of digital data, now sent streaming across space towards the planet Earth.

Greta Zargo opened her eyes.
    She yawned.
    She shivered.

She felt like she was just waking up after a long sleep in a cold place.

She looked around.

She was in a tiny room.

And then the wall in front of her hissed and lifted itself away, opening up and offering Greta her first sight of another world.

She stepped out, stretching and yawning again.

She was in a big domed tent.

She felt new and fresh and light.

She bounced on her toes.

She was definitely lighter than she had been.

What had happened?

She remembered climbing into a cabinet ... and ...

Oh!

She was looking for her aunt … that was
it …

'Aunt Tabitha?' she called.

Aunt Tabitha didn't answer, being,
currently, a stream of disembodied data
winging its way across the solar system.

CHAPTER SIXTEEN

Upper Lowerbridge, England, Earth

LAST SATURDAY (EARLY EVENING)

THE AMOEBA MONSTER had never felt rain before.

This feeling of *tip-tap-tap* on its outer membrane was fascinating.

It was like nothing it had ever felt, but had it had the vocabulary it would have compared it to sparrows tap-dancing happiness or fingers pretend-typing love notes

or small drops of water pitter-pattering.

Of course, that last simile would be the most accurate one, because that's exactly what it was, except ... not *just* that.

When the shell from Field Marshall Herbert's tank had bounced off the highly elastic and impenetrably tough outer membrane of the amoeba monster that had eaten Mr Jamali, it had landed plumb on Aunt Tabitha's Inventing Shed.

Aunt Tabitha's Inventing Shed had been filling with gas ever since Greta Zargo had accidentally and unknowingly knocked the jar of Know-It-All Brain Food into the gas spigot on the workbench.

Explosive shells and combustible gases are not the happiest of friends, so as soon as they met, they had an argument of sorts, which is to say there was yet another almighty *BANG!* and the contents of Aunt Tabitha's Inventing Shed (and the shed itself) were sent flying high into the air, to rain down as ash and small bits of wreckage over the whole of Upper Lowerbridge.

In the explosion, the Know-It-All Brain Food jar was shattered into tiny fragments and the Know-It-All Brain Food became a very fine hot mist of very clever chemical compounds that were absorbed into the clouds above.

With all the upset, they then began to rain.

And it was this rain, mainly ordinary water but containing drops of Know-It-All Brain Food, that was dancing across the membrane of the amoeba monster.

Deep inside the jelly swam the skeleton of a cat.

And inside the skull of the skeleton of the cat, wobbled the cat's brain.*

As the Know-It-All Brain Food in the rain was absorbed through the creature's outer membrane, something strange began to happen.

For the first time in its entire life, after long millennia of living underground and

* The brain, housed inside the indigestible skull, was the last piece of the cat the amoeba monster could eat. Its jelly lapped at it slowly, probing through the small holes at the base of the skull and where the optic nerves went from the eyes. Had those holes been bigger, the brain would have been eaten sooner. Perhaps too soon.

short hours of living in the light, the amoeba monster had a thought.

Meow, it thought, oddly.

Instead of a series of vague nerve bundles spread throughout the jelly-like blob of the thing, it was, for the first time, using a tight cluster of nerve cells. After all these long ages the amoeba monster had *a brain*.

It was a cat's brain, granted, and it was thinking cattish thoughts, admittedly, and it didn't realise it was anything other than a cat, but still, in a very real sense it was … well, it was a bit of a muddle.

Meow, it thought again.

It tried to scratch an itch behind its ear, without realising that it didn't have an ear, nor a leg to scratch the ear that wasn't there with.

And the amoeba monster that had swallowed the cat, Major Influence, wasn't the only amoeba monster that was changing.

The one that had swallowed Jessica Plumb was thinking: *Oh, it's raining. I wonder what would happen if you made clouds out of soap? You'd be able just to go outside to have a shower. But you'd have to take your clothes off in the garden and that's probably a bit weird. I bet my mum and dad would never allow it, the old fuddy-duddies …*

The one that had swallowed Oscar Teachbaddly was thinking: *The school holidays never last as long as you imagine they will. When I was a boy they went on for years and years, but then I was an awful truant. After all, that's why mum and dad are in prison. I ought to go and visit them this holiday, but …*

The one that had swallowed Mrs Jamali was thinking: *I can't believe the dentist did it. It seems far too obvious. Maybe I'll try a different book next time. This one wasn't as good as I'd hoped …*

The one that had swallowed PC Delinquent was thinking: *I wonder what's for tea.*

The one that had swallowed Susan Terrapin was thinking: *I wonder what noise terrapins make. I've been a terrapin for years and*

I've not worked it out yet. Maybe tomorrow I'll try
saying 'Woof'. Maybe that's it ...

A whole rash of thinking was breaking
out all over Upper Lowerbridge.

But that wasn't the only thing that was
happening.

CHAPTER SEVENTEEN

Hester Sometimes Conference Centre and Immobile Library, Near Upper Lowerbridge, England, Earth

LAST SATURDAY (EVENING)

AFTER GRETA HAD been disassembled by the Teleport Booth, Yevgeny Ticklenesser had waited and watched the flashing lights and listened to the hum of the machine as it transmitted Greta towards the sky.

And then absolutely nothing happened for more than half an hour.

And then something happened.

New lights began flashing and the machine started humming and rumbling with different noises, and something started *being made* inside the cabinet. Smoke wreathed and lightning flared and atoms bonded with other atoms, and slowly the shape of a human could be seen coming together through the little window in the front of the Teleport Booth.

But because nothing had happened for so long, Yevgeny Ticklenesser had gone to sleep and didn't see the miracle of information-rich atomic recombination happening.

Eventually the door opened with a hiss and Aunt Tabitha stepped out.

'Home at last!' she said, stretching and yawning.

It took it out of you, this being reduced to digital data in one place and being rebuilt atom by atom in another place. She felt like she could do with a lie down.

But instead of lying down, Aunt Tabitha tapped gently on Ticklenesser's reverse diving suit and asked the octopus, when he woke up and uncoiled his tentacles, what time it was.

When Ticklenesser had told her the

correct time he said, 'Aunt Tabitha, good to see you back. Returned. Your short human, Greta, with you?'

'Greta? Why would Greta be with me?'

'She went through glowing fish machine, go find you.'

'Oh, heck,' said Aunt Tabitha.

She climbed back into the machine and the door hissed shut behind her and she pressed the button labelled 'Go!' and was flash-frozen and deconstructed by lasers and reduced to a pile of Undifferentiated Atomic Dust and transmitted through space back to the matching Teleport Booth on Mars.

On Mars, Greta Zargo had looked everywhere she could think of for her aunt and not found her.

There were no space suits there that fitted a girl of her size,* and so she couldn't go and check the rest of Mars outside the dome,★ which was fine, because there was ⟶ a lot of it and it would take an awfully long time. Also, she didn't think Aunt Tabitha was out there, because there were the same number of spacesuits as there were spacesuit pegs, which suggested Aunt Tabitha wasn't currently wearing a spacesuit, unless they'd brought more spacesuits than they had pegs, which seemed silly.

She suddenly remembered the book that Hester Sometimes had given her with a wink, and pulled it out of her pocket eagerly. Maybe, she thought, the *Girl's Guide to Mars* was exactly what she needed right now … Maybe that old woman *had* worked wonders

* it wasn't that Greta was short for her age, she always said, but rather, she maintained, that she was old for her height.

★ She had worked out where she was through a combination of looking at the red dusty landscape outside the dome, bouncing on her toes in the slightly lower gravity and reading the labels on the tinned peaches, which said: Mars Mission Peaches, specially canned for the BASA Mars Mission by Mars Mission Canning Company.

from the other side, giving her this special clue …

But when she opened the *Girl's Guide to Mars* and thumbed through it, it turned out to be a book about the Roman god, not the planet, which was less useful than she'd hoped. (Hester Sometimes clearly was just a mad, old, occasionally dead lady who'd *almost* got lucky with the random book she'd grabbed to get rid of Greta with.)

So, after twenty minutes of looking around, nibbling a few crackers and gazing through the transparent dome at another planet, she climbed back into the Teleport Booth and pressed the button labelled 'Go!'.

She was immediately flash-frozen, deconstructed by lasers, reduced to a pile of Undifferentiated Atomic Dust and transmitted through space back to the

matching Teleport Booth in the Hester Sometimes Conference Centre and Immobile Library.

When Aunt Tabitha was reconstructed for a second time on Mars, from the Undifferentiated Atomic Dust store kept in the large tank beneath the Teleport Booth*, ⤷

* Which happened just as soon as the machine had finished disassembling Greta's atoms. The booth was only big enough, after all, to fit one person in at a time.

she had a quick look around the domed city and found that Greta wasn't there.

She counted the spacesuits carefully, and looked out of the airlock window, just in case.

She wondered if the octopus had lied to her for some *nefarious** reason, but then she threw the idea away. She'd met Ticklenesser before, back in his own under-sea city at the Eleventh Annual Festival of New Stuff (EAFoNS, for short), and he'd been a very nice chap. She still used the clockwork kettle that he had invented to make her morning cup of tea.

He must have been telling her the truth, but she'd been *too slow*.

So she climbed back into the cabinet, pressed the button and was teleported back to Earth.

* Aunt Tabitha already knew this word, and in fact Mildred Mildred had learnt it from her at the Ninth Annual Festival of New Stuff (NAFoNS, for short), when she'd said, 'It makes a nice change for nothing nefarious to be happening this year, don't you think?'.

*   *   *

Meanwhile, Greta arrived on Earth to be
told by Ticklenesser that her Aunt Tabitha
had been on Mars but had come back to
Earth when Greta had gone to Mars to look
for her, but that she had then gone back to
Mars to find Greta, and so Greta climbed
back into the Teleport Booth and pressed
the button labelled 'Go!' and …

CHAPTER EIGHTEEN

Upper Lowerbridge, England, Earth

LAST SATURDAY (SUPPER TIME)

JESSICA PLUMB WOKE up, naked, chilly and in a duck pond.

Up above her, stars twinkled through ragged holes in the dark clouds.

She didn't normally fall asleep in duck ponds, and she couldn't remember how she'd got there.

As she pulled ducks and duck weed from

her hair she thought: *It's a mystery. I'll have to tell Greta about it. Maybe she'll be able to solve it.*

And then she thought: *I wonder what time it is. It's dark, but then it gets dark early these days, it being the autumn. I hope it's not very late, or Mum and Dad will be in a big worry.*

Fashioning a rudimentary garment out of some large lily pads, she set off home.

But it turned out her parents weren't in a big worry. They were in the garden, naked. (Luckily there were a pair of small shrubs that hid their 'embarrassment' – and their 'bits'.)

'Hi, Mum. Hi, Dad,' Jessica said as she pushed open the gate. 'What are you doing out here?'

Her mum and dad looked at each other

and, wiping a bit of jelly off their faces, said, 'Dunno.'

They all went inside, got dressed, had some cheese on toast and promised one another never to mention this evening again.

Field Marshall Gwendoline Herbert woke up in the turret of her tank, naked.

She tried to remember why she'd parked

it in the street outside her sister's house, but her mind drew a blank.

Wiping a bit of jelly out of her ear she lifted the tank's controller in her hand and, as quietly as she could, reversed out of town before anyone noticed her.

PC Delinquent woke up in the Brigadier's back garden, out of uniform.

He was lucky enough to find his helmet lying on the grass nearby and quickly put it on as he wondered what had happened.

Wiping some jellyish stuff from between his toes, he tried to work out why he was where he was, dressed as he was. He remembered *something* about the Brigadier. He'd been called to come and have a word with the cantankerous old fellow about *something*, again, but his memory was foggy on the details. And after that ... nothing.

Since it was dark and the Brigadier seemed not to be causing anyone any trouble, PC Delinquent walked home.

Halfway up the street he passed the Cohens coming the other way, also stark naked, as if they were going home after a night out at the nudist theatre. He lifted his hat politely and said, 'Good evening.'

After passing the time of the day for a few minutes, they all agreed it was getting a little nippy, and so they went their separate ways having seen *nothing odd at all*.

Major Influence (who was also completely naked, though furry) shook the last of the jelly from his tail and ate a mouse that had been pulling faces at what it had thought was a sleeping cat.

After eating the mouse, he hopped up on to the remaining upright bit of fence and began to sing.

What had happened was this.

The Know-It-All Brain Food had been absorbed by the amoeba monsters.

The brains inside the skulls inside the amoeba monsters had been given a super kickstart by the Know-It-All.

All cells contain the blueprint for the creature they belong to (it's all there in the DNA if you look close enough). The cells of these kickstarted brains sent out messages into the jelly-like blobs that they floated in the middle of.

The amoeba monsters, having no brains

of their own, had no defence against these new instructions.

The creatures' own cells followed the new instructions* and grew themselves into ⤴ hearts and hair and spleens and toenails and lungs and eyeballs and all that sort of stuff (but not clothes, because no one's DNA codes for clothing).

And so, over the course of a couple of hours, each and every amoeba monster that had swallowed someone had become that person. Not *a copy* of that person, but *that person* themselves.

And, for whatever reason, their brains forgot the time they were inside the jelly, and although some people in the months that followed had odd, naked, wobbly dreams, no one ever mentioned them, assuming they were the only ones who'd woken up naked

* Quite possibly because 'Grow some arms and legs and whathaveyous' was a more interesting instruction than 'Be blobby'.

213

on a Saturday night, out of doors and covered with a few globules of jelly.

When Greta's old infant school teacher, Oscar Teachbaddly, woke up, dribbling a little jelly from his nose, he found himself completely nude and halfway up a lamppost.

He assumed Julian and Barry and Simon and Clive and Petros and Aaron and Sebastian and Esteban and Andrew and Big Derek and Sarah and Little Derek and Ivan and Sandra had played a prank on him. It wouldn't be the first time.

He grumbled as he climbed down and made his way home.

He was upset to see that several parts of his wheelbarrow-based front garden had been knocked over and said three words that (a) Greta could never print in the newspaper and (b) would get a teacher sacked if they said any of them in the classroom.

'Just wait until Julian and Barry and Simon and Clive and Petros and Aaron and Sebastian and Esteban and Andrew and Big Derek and Sarah and Little Derek and Ivan and Sandra get home. I'm going to give them a piece of my mind,'* he said, ⤵ mostly to himself, but also a little bit to the world at large.

* Probably piece number sixteen, which just goes to show how angry he was.

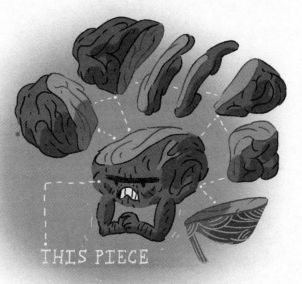

THIS PIECE

But he never got the chance to give anything to them, because they never came home again.*

*Since Mr Teachbaddly had a teacher's brain, it was bigger and more powerful than any of the others' brains, and so, when the amoeba monster that contained him and Julian and Barry and Simon and Clive and Petros and Aaron and Sebastian and Esteban and Andrew and Big Derek and Sarah and Little Derek and Ivan and Sandra absorbed the Know-It-All and began to grow into something new, it was his brain that took charge.

CHAPTER NINETEEN

Hester Sometimes Conference Centre and Immobile Library, Near Upper Lowerbridge, England, Earth

LAST SUNDAY (BRUNCH TIME)

GRETA AND JESSICA sat in the audience in the Hester Sometimes Conference Centre and Immobile Library's main hall and listened to the presentations and demonstrations of the handful of scientists and inventors who hadn't been able to get taxis home the day before.

The Bellerophon brothers and clone chased miniature ostriches round the stage, but the birds refused to lay any eggs, which was a little disappointing for them.

Walbur P. Buffalo had Simon do her business on stage and then cooked the burger that had emerged on a little portable clockwork frying pan (which was Yevgeny Ticklenesser's invention for this year). When he asked for a volunteer from the audience to taste it (it *did* smell good), Greta, who quite fancied trying a bite in order to be able to write about it accurately in the article she was composing,* let Jessica go up on stage, since she'd missed out on all the excitement of the previous day.*

* She was secretly hoping it tasted like what normally comes out the back end of a cow, so that she could be mean and dismissive when she wrote it up, since she didn't much like Mr Walbur P. Buffalo.

* Jessica declared it, 'A little grassy, but not at all unpleasant.'.

218

Arthur Rumble presented a goldfish that could remember your name.

China Bloggs demonstrated a machine that could turn unwanted phone calls from people trying to sell you encyclopaedias or unnecessarily expensive watering cans into a lightly perfumed wind that could power a small turbine, providing enough energy (per phone call) to power a lawnmower for five seconds.

Rupi Ionesco showed off a pair of trousers that could remember your way home.

Hollie Quirkstandard had invented an apple that glowed in the dark and cured paper cuts.

Greta *had* expected Aunt Tabitha to end the event with her amazing Teleport Booth, but instead she displayed a hat that always pointed north. When Greta asked her afterwards why she hadn't presented the Teleport Booth, her aunt said to her and Jessica, 'I think we've had quite enough of that for now!'

And they'd all laughed, even though Jessica didn't know what exactly they were laughing at, since no one had explained it to her yet.*

* But since people always laughed at something someone said at the end of Jessica's favourite television programmes, for example, Space Adventures in Space or Inventor Godot's Accidental Triumph or The Time-Travelling Joneses, she didn't mind joining in at all. It made her feel a part of the gang.

POSTLOGUE

IT HAD BEEN gone midnight, Earth time, before Greta and her aunt had stopped chasing one another across the solar system.

They'd eaten crackers and peaches together under the Martian sky (under the dome), watching the sun set small and white beyond the distant red hills.

When they'd got back to Upper Lowerbridge a few hours later, Aunt Tabitha noticed that her Inventing Shed had exploded and Greta said it had been nothing to do with her.*

In the morning, as they cycled back to the Hester Sometimes Conference Centre and

*She didn't mention the fact that Jessica had said she was going to look in the Inventing Shed too, because she didn't want to get her friend in trouble.

221

Immobile Library, they noticed that the town was in a bit of a state – fences were knocked down, lampposts were bent at odd angles, a few cars seemed to have been squashed, Greta's garden had grown a distinct slope and the Brigadier looked thirty years younger and waved warmly with a smile as they went past.

'I think my shed caused a bit more havoc when it blew up than I thought,' said Aunt Tabitha. 'I'd best write Wilfred a letter that he can put in the paper. You know, an apology.'

The letter was published a week later, alongside Greta's article on the weekend's adventure: INVENTOR GOES MISSING AT INVENTORS' MEETUP BECAUSE OF VACUUM CLEANER PLUG CONFUSION CAUSED BY STUPID CLEANER.*

In the article, Greta described the inventions on show and told readers which one

* Wilf Inglebath tidied the headline up for publication, mainly by removing the bit about Mrs Hummock, who was his sister-in-law and whom he had to spend time with at weddings, birthday parties and swimming lessons.

had been presented with the Big Golden Rosette of Science and Technology, as voted for by the scientists and inventors present at the Twelfth Annual Festival of New Stuff (TAFoNS, for short), by a proud and grinning Jessica Plumb (who had counted the votes), while at the same time being quite rude about its inventor.*

* It was Walbur P. Buffalo, of course.

A few weeks after that, Greta received a rather soggy postcard from Yevgeny Ticklenesser to thank her for sending him a copy of the newspaper that she'd had Aunt Tabitha laminate for him. At least, she assumed it was from Ticklenesser, but the ink had run.

She put it on the table where she was eating her breakfast on the first day back at school.

It was half past nine and she was late, but she wasn't worried.

After all, she was Greta Zargo: a star newspaper reporter who was friends with an octopus, an aunt and a girl two doors down, who was the first eleven-year-old girl to accidentally travel to Mars (eleven times (or had it been twelve?)), and who was having sherbet scrambled eggs on toast, which were causing her mouth to foam a little at the edges … And you know what? It really wasn't such a bad thing to be.

The Head would just have to be patient.

Greta would get there soon.

In her own time.

And when she did, boy, did she have one great 'What I did in the autumn half-term holiday' essay to write.

But, she smiled, ungrudgingly, spooning another spoonful of fizzing egg into her mouth, *that can wait another hour or two*. And she thought of Clause 5 of her parents' Last Will and Testament, which said: *Greta, darling, there's no need to rush all the time, and never complain about the size of your shoes to a travelling nun, unless she smells slightly of pickled gherkins.**

Yes. She liked being Greta Zargo.

* Mainly she thought of the first part of Clause Five, since her shoes were quite comfortable, thank you very much for asking.

COULD YOU BE A REPORTER LIKE GRETA?

WERE YOU PAYING ATTENTION?

TAKE THIS QUIZ AND FIND OUT!

1. Where did Aunt Tabitha go missing from?

a) The Hester Sometimes Conference Centre and Immobile Library

b) Her Inventing Shed

c) Your house

2. The first inventor/scientist Greta questioned had what type of animal with him?

a) A spoon

b) A miniature ostrich

c) A cow

3. How did Greta know who Yevgeny Ticklenesser was?

a) He was wearing a name badge

b) She solved a mysterious riddle set by a mythical monster

c) It was written on a bit of paper inside a fortune cookie

4. How many Bellerophon Triplets are there?

a) 3

b) 57

c) 0 – technically there are the Bellerophon Twins and their cloned brother

5. What did Hester Sometimes give Greta to help her solve the mystery?

a) A book

b) A funny look

c) A waterproof cake

6. **Who was the last person who saw Aunt Tabitha before she vanished?**

a) Agnes Nottin-Thisbok

b) Mrs Hummock

c) Bellerophon Alpha

7. **What important clue did Greta discover in Aunt Tabitha's inventing shed?**

a) The blueprints for her invention

b) Aunt Tabitha

c) A footprint shaped like a spoon

8. **What was Aunt Tabitha's invention?**

a) A Teleport Booth

b) King Magnus III, Lord of Spoons

c) A mysterious riddle set by a mythical monster

9. **Where was Aunt Tabitha?**

a) Just over there

b) No, just over there

c) On Mars

10. **Who won the Big Golden Rosette of Science and Technology at the Twelfth Annual Festival of New Stuff?**

a) Agnes Nottin-Thisbok

b) Walbur P. Buffalo

c) You, the wise and wonderful reader - congratulations

MADE WITH - COWPAT- PATTIES

LOOK OUT FOR GRETA'S OTHER ADVENTURE IN:

OUT NOW!

Turn over for a sneak peek and see what
Greta gets up to next ...

PROLOGUE

Earth

LAST SUNDAY

N O ONE ON Earth knew that their planet was being observed.

No one realised that vast computer brains waited, hidden in high Earth orbit, plotting and planning the planet's destruction.

No one detected the silvery robot as it descended from the blue summer's sky with a slow, quiet whoosh of unknown energy and flew towards the small English town of Middling Otherbridge.

No one knew that only three things stood in the way of their complete and utter annihilation: one elderly parrot, one eleven-year-old spelling mistake and one intrepid young newspaper-reporter-cum-schoolgirl in search of a Big Scoop.

And yet, that's exactly what's at stake in this book: *the fate of the entire planet Earth*.

Now read on ...

CHAPTER ONE

Upper Lowerbridge, England, Earth

LAST MONDAY

WHEN GRETA ZARGO'S parents accidentally died she was left the family home, everything in it, a large bank account, a library card, three hamsters (now dead, stuffed and on the mantelpiece), a lifetime subscription to *Clipboarding Weekly* magazine (*the* magazine for all clipboarding enthusiasts) and a pair of scissors she was to never run with. Since she had only been a baby at the time, all of this was held in trust for her by her Aunt Tabitha until her eighth birthday.*

As soon as she turned eight Greta moved out of her aunt's house and into her own one, just over the road. Naturally her aunt kept an eye on Greta, whenever she remembered to, and in the three years that followed absolutely no disasters had occurred. Other than perhaps that one time the fire engine had to come to get her off the roof. But even then, as Greta pointed out in a stiffly worded letter to the school newspaper, she hadn't *actually* been stuck. So, no disasters at all.

It was in the bathroom of that very house that Greta Zargo was now hiding underneath the bubbles in a deep, hot bath she'd

* The relevant sentence in her parents' Last Will and Testament should, of course, have read 'eighteenth birthday' but contained a legally binding spelling mistake. (It should be noted that this is not the spelling mistake mentioned in the Prologue; that's a different one made around the same time.)

run for herself. She soaked in the steaming tub, and breathed deep of the foamy perfume. This wasn't the best idea since it tickled her nose and made her sneeze, which blew a hole in the bubbles through which she could see the bathroom ceiling.

The ceiling, being a little grey at the edges, reminded her of her disappointing morning.

It was the summer and, being a girl of sparky determination, she'd got herself a holiday job as a Very Junior Reporter for *The Local Newspaper*.* It wasn't a real holiday job, since there are laws against employing eleven-year-old children, but when she'd followed Mr Inglebath (the newspaper's editor) across the park, through the library and into the swimming pool, asking to work for him, she had seemed so like a girl who

* *The Local Newspaper* was an award-winning newspaper, as it proudly boasted on the front cover. It had won the Most Accurately Titled Print Periodical Prize four years running, until the Adverts for Old Fridges (Incorporating Gossip & Photos of Local People) Weekly beat it to the top spot last time round.

wouldn't take no for an answer that he'd said yes.

He quickly explained, however, that he wasn't going to pay her (though she was welcome to a biscuit or two whenever she visited the office).

This was fine by Greta. She wasn't in it for the money.

She had bought herself a new reporter's notebook and her aunt had made her a press badge with a tiny tape recorder hidden inside it.

When you pressed the button labelled 'Press' on the press badge it recorded everything it heard, which meant she didn't need to use the reporter's notebook to take notes, unless the press badge had run out of batteries, which it sometimes did. So, with the press badge pinned to her jacket and the notebook in her bag, just in case, she was ready to go out and report the news.

Oh, she had been so excited, and then …

The problem was that as a Very Junior Reporter it was her job to go where her editor sent her and to cover the stories he told her to cover. That was just the way of things, and this morning Mr Inglebath had sent her to talk to Hari Socket about his missing Battenberg cake (he'd bought it for his son's birthday and had taken it out of the wrapper and put it on a plate in the kitchen from where it had mysteriously vanished while he was watching *Stop! Look! Redecorate!* in the front room). It had taken Greta two minutes and twenty-three seconds of investigation for her to realise this was *a rubbish story*. This was not *front page material*, and never would be, not unless a whole lot more cakes went missing, and what was the likelihood of that happening?